"Alex?" Weston spoke again, his voice slow and deep and way too sexy.

"Hmm?"

"You ever plan on answering my question?"

"Absolutely." It came out sounding aggressive, almost angry. She made herself speak more cordially. "Yes. Honestly. There's plenty of room here. You're staying in the cottage. It's settled."

"You're so bossy..." He said that all slow, too—slow and kind of naughty, and she sincerely hoped her cheeks weren't cherry red.

"Weston." She said his name sternly, as a rebuke.

"Alexandra," he mocked.

"That's a yes, right?" Now she made her voice pleasant, even a little too sweet. "You'll take the second bedroom."

"Yes, I will. And it's good to talk to you, Alex. At last." Did he really have to be so...ironic? It wasn't like she hadn't thought more than once about reaching out to him, checking in with him to see how he was holding up. But back in January, when they'd said goodbye, he'd seemed totally on board with cutting it clean. "Alex? You still there?"

"Uh, yes. Great."

"See you day after tomorrow. I'll be flying down with Easton."

"Perfect. See you then." She heard the click as he disconnected the call.

Dear Reader,

Life. Too bad it rarely goes according to plan. You can do everything right, plan for every emergency, scrimp and save and be ready for the worst sort of "rainy day." And then what happens? Life throws you a curveball and all your planning and working and saving turn out to mean zip.

For Alexandra Hererra, it's suddenly time to go home to Wild Rose Farm and figure out what to do with the rest of her life.

The good news? Alex has her own little cottage all to herself on the family farm. She can spend the holidays sitting around in her reindeer pajamas streaming shows she never had time to watch before, eating way too much ice cream straight from the carton while she figures out what in the world to do next.

However, there is one little problem: Alex's perfect little cottage is the only one on the farm with a bedroom to spare and someone else in her extended family needs a place to stay for the holidays... Someone hunky and charming, someone with whom Alex has a bit of a secret history: her sister's husband's twin brother, Weston Wright.

It's not how she wanted it. But what can she say?

I can't believe we're on book three of the Wild Rose Sisters trilogy. Each one has been such fun to write. I hope you enjoy Alex and West's story, and that your own upcoming holidays are full of family, love and good cheer.

Happy reading, everyone!

Christine

The Christmas Cottage

CHRISTINE RIMMER

ISBN-13: 978-1-335-72425-0

The Christmas Cottage

For questions and comments about the quality of this book, please contact us at CustomerService@Harlequin.com.

Harlequin Enterprises ULC
22 Adelaide St. West, 41st Floor
Toronto, Ontario M5H 4E3, Canada
www.Harlequin.com

Printed in U.S.A.

Christine Rimmer came to her profession the long way around. She tried everything from acting to teaching to telephone sales. Now she's finally found work that suits her perfectly. She insists she never had a problem keeping a job—she was merely gaining "life experience" for her future as a novelist. Christine lives with her family in Oregon. Visit her at christinerimmer.com.

Books by Christine Rimmer

Harlequin Special Edition

Wild Rose Sisters

The Father of Her Sons
First Comes Baby...

The Bravos of Valentine Bay

Almost a Bravo
Same Time, Next Christmas
Switched at Birth
A Husband She Couldn't Forget
The Right Reason to Marry
Their Secret Summer Family
Home for the Baby's Sake
A Temporary Christmas Arrangement
The Last One Home

Montana Mavericks: Brothers & Broncos

Summer Nights with the Maverick

Montana Mavericks:
The Real Cowboys of Bronco Heights

The Rancher's Summer Secret

Visit the Author Profile page
at Harlequin.com for more titles.

This one's for Annmarie Anderson and her senior citizen shih tzu mix, StarBaby. StarBaby is the inspiration for the rescue dog, Cookie, who is adopted by the heroine in this book.

I asked Annmarie to share a little about StarBaby. She said, "StarBaby is an old lady shelter dog. She likes to cuddle and eat her Cesar dog food. She weighs eight pounds. I talk to her all the time but she averts her eyes and won't answer. I love her with all my heart."

Chapter One

Up until the moment she cracked open that fortune cookie, Alexandra Herrera had no clue that her life was about to change in a very big way.

A hard-charging career woman, Alex was a true rising star at the Portland law offices of Kauffman, Judd and Tisdale. She was crushing it and everyone at the firm knew it, too.

Two months from now, in January, one of the longtime partners would finally retire. Alex would be stepping up to take his place. And not as a junior partner. Oh, no. She would make full partner at the age of thirty-three, one with equity in the firm. Because a non-equity partnership had never been an option. Not for Alex. She wanted it all—and not only the fancy title. She wanted a partner's share of the power and the profits, and she would get what she wanted. To that end, she had worked relentlessly, scrimping and saving to pay off her student loans and then to fund her buy-in once she made partner.

A successful lawyer enjoyed financial security, prestige and the possibility she might contribute to making the world a better place. Alex had grown up hungry for those things, and by her sophomore year in high school, she'd had her dreams for her future nailed down. She'd graduated from USC at the top of her class and received her JD from Berkeley, magna cum laude, law review.

She had it all going her way—except for just one little problem. One tiny, annoying issue that wouldn't quit niggling at the back of her mind: lately, she couldn't stop thinking about her father.

On the first day of June, nearly six months ago now, Leandro Herrera, eighty-three and supposedly in great shape for his age, had suffered a heart attack on the golf course at the Los Angeles Country Club. He'd died in an ambulance on the way to Cedars-Sinai. Leandro had left everything to Alex in his will—the houses, the cars, the enormous stock portfolio. Even the airplane.

No worries about funding her buy-in now.

She ought to be thrilled. She wasn't.

It bothered her a lot, to be shunted aside for three decades and then suddenly discover she'd inherited a fortune from the virtual stranger who had provided half her DNA.

Now, on the Monday before Thanksgiving, as she sat down at her desk to a working take-out lunch of General Tso's chicken, all that money Leandro had left her popped into her conscious mind again. Mentally, she swatted it away. It pissed her off royally, it really did. To have lost the dad she'd hardly known and in his place, to have a pile of money fall on her—more money than she would ever be likely to spend in her lifetime.

It felt all wrong to her. It felt like everything bad, like betrayal and futility, a lifetime of planning and working and *trying* just going up in smoke. It felt like the awful growing awareness that, had she only known there would always be plenty of money, had she known that her sisters and her beloved aunt would never lose the family farm where she'd been raised…had she understood that no matter what kind of mess she made of her life, if money were needed to save someone she loved, Alex would end up more than able to provide it…

Had she only known that her dad would leave her everything, well, she certainly wouldn't have spent the past eight years clawing her way up the food chain at Kauffman, Judd and Tisdale.

Alex flipped back the lid of the take-out container and stared at her lunch.

"Uh-uh." She covered the meal again and pushed it aside, then stuck her hand in the bag and grabbed a fortune cookie—an odd move for her. Alex never ate fortune cookies. She never even broke them open to read what was inside. She was master of her life and her fate, which meant that she could not care less what some fortune cookie had to say.

Today, though…

That cookie called to her somehow. Crumbs littered her desk pad as she cracked it open to get to the scrap of paper within. Smoothing the white strip, she read her fortune.

Do it now.

Blinking in an odd combination of shock and puzzlement, she read it again, out loud this time. "Do it now…"

A direct instruction.

She scoffed. No fortune cookie gave direct instructions. It was always a prediction or generalized advice couched in open-ended terms.

Do it now.

The scrape of her own chair startled her as she shoved it back. And then she was moving, walking out of her office. Her assistant, Maude, rose from her desk, asking, "Everything okay, Alex?" as she went by.

Alex answered vaguely with a wave of one hand, "Fine, Maude. No worries…" and kept on walking.

Grant Judd, second in line to the managing partner, and Alex's mentor and immediate supervisor at KJ&T, was just exiting his office.

"A moment, Grant?" She put a question mark at the end, but it wasn't a question.

"I've got lunch with Alan Riker in twenty minutes." Riker was an important client.

"This won't take long." She swept into his office.

He followed, shutting the door. "This had better be important, Alex." There was disappointment in his tone.

And why wouldn't there be? She knew better than to sidetrack her boss when a big client was waiting. Grant had mentored her because she was one step ahead of every other associate all the time. Because she never said no to anything that helped the firm. Because she networked with the best of them. She got along with everyone from paralegals to partners and she could work a room like nobody's business.

She had a knack for retaining existing clients and finding new ones, too. Alex was the only associate with her own assistant and she had earned the admirable, smart-as-a-whip Maude because whatever KJ&T needed, Alex worked hard to make happen. She took on every challenge thrown at her and she did it with confidence, flair and a smile on her face.

Not today, though.

Today, she kept her expression cool and distant. She looked Grant Judd square in the eye—and committed career suicide. "Something's come up, Grant." *Something in a cookie.* "I quit."

At her apartment two hours later, after being escorted from the office by the nice security guard named Lester, Alex packed up her SUV and headed for the family farm.

Wild Rose Farm was an hour's drive east from Portland and not far from Alex's hometown of Heartwood. Alex's mother's family, the Dahls, had owned the farm for generations.

Over the past seventy years or so, various Dahls had built three houses on the farm—three houses arranged in a circle around a broad, gently sloping central yard. The first house along the graveled driveway from the main road belonged to Payton Wright, Alex's youngest half sister. Married last New Year's Day to the father of her twin sons, Payton lived in Seattle now with her husband, Easton, and their boys, but she came home to Wild Rose often.

When Alex arrived at a little after six that night, all the lights were on at Payton's cottage. Alex pulled in at the end of the front walk. She was hurrying up the steps in the drizzling icy rain when the door swung open and her five-year-old twin nephews tumbled out.

"Aunt Alex!" Penn, older than Bailey by several minutes, threw himself at her.

"Hey there…" She crouched on the porch to return his hug, holding out an arm to catch Bailey in a three-way embrace.

Bailey shouted over his shoulder, "Mom! Aunt Alex is here!"

Alex hugged both boys hard and breathed in their wonderful puppy-dog smell.

Payton, her hair piled in a messy topknot and her belly looking about to pop, appeared in the open doorway wearing an expression of disbelief. "Alex?"

Alex offered weakly, "Surprise?"

"Three days early. I can hardly believe my eyes." Payton held out her arms. The boys jumped around them as the sisters shared a hug of greeting.

Alex pulled back to fondly pat the bulge of her sister's stomach. "How's my niece?" The baby was due January 12.

"Active," replied Payton. "Just like her big brothers—you hungry?"

All of a sudden, Alex realized she was starving. "Yes! What are we having?"

"Turkey sloppy joes and crinkly fries!" crowed Bailey.

Penn added his endorsement. "Sloppy joes are the best!"

Payton gently clasped Alex's shoulder. "Everything okay?"

"Good. Fine. I'm actually hoping to take over the guest cottage for more than a couple of days this time." The next house along the driveway used to be Josie's cottage. But in April, their middle half sister had married Miles Halstead, who owned the farm next door. Josie and her baby son, Davy, had moved in with Miles and his two teenage daughters. Now Josie and Miles worked both farms as a team. And over the Fourth of July weekend at a family meeting, Alex, Payton, Josie and their aunt Marilyn had unanimously agreed to repurpose Josie's cottage for guests.

"The guest cottage is ready and waiting just for you," Payton confirmed as the boys dodged around them and entered the house. "Auntie M and Ernesto are here already."

"Great." Nowadays, Aunt Marilyn lived with her boyfriend, Ernesto Bezzini, in Salinas. Ernesto owned an artichoke farm there.

Payton wore a worried frown. "Tell me what's going on."

Alex just went ahead and said it. "I quit my job today."

Her sister's mouth dropped open. "You didn't..."

"Oh, yes, I did."

Payton shivered a little and rewrapped her big sweater around her giant baby bump. "You're okay, though...?"

"I am. I think."

Payton pulled her close again and whispered, "We need a family meeting. Tonight. You can tell us everything."

"Yes, I—"

Bailey stuck his head out the door. "Mom. My tummy is *growling...*"

So they went inside and Payton dished up the sloppy joes. Once everyone had eaten, Ernesto came over to keep an eye on the twins while Alex, Payton, Josie and Aunt Marilyn convened in the guest cottage.

The place looked great, Alex thought with pride. Back last summer after she'd received her whopping unexpected inheritance, Alex had insisted that the repurposed cottage needed a new roof, siding and windows. She'd had the place freshly painted inside and out and redone the kitchen and bathroom. She'd also bought furniture to replace the pieces Josie had taken with her to her new home at Halstead Farm.

In the kitchen with its pretty granite counters

and glass tile backsplashes, Josie whipped up hot chocolate while Alex told the story of what a fortune cookie made her do.

"Did you save it?" demanded Payton.

"My fortune? Yes, I did. It was still on my desk pad along with a few cookie crumbs when I started packing up my sad cardboard box of personal possessions. I taped it to an index card." She pulled the card from her pocket, and they passed it around.

Shaking her curly head, Josie read the three simple words. *"Do it now."*

"And you did," Auntie M, slim and strong as ever in faded jeans and a big white sweater, declared proudly. "And I think it's wonderful. It was the right move for you. You've outgrown that job."

"Or maybe I've just lost my mind…"

"Not a chance," said Josie.

Payton insisted, "A whole new life is opening up for you, Alex. I just know it."

"Well, one thing's for sure." Alex took a big gulp of her hot chocolate, which she'd liberally fortified with Baileys Irish Cream. "No matter what happens next, it's not as though I'll starve."

Josie stepped close and wrapped an arm around Alex's shoulders. "I'm sorry your dad's gone. I know you miss him."

Alex tried not to roll her eyes. "Hard to miss what you never had."

"My darling." Auntie M put an arm around her from the other side. "I'm thinking you need to keep your options open for a while."

Josie was nodding. "You deserve a real break, time to relax and recharge, time to think through what you're going to do next. You've worked nonstop since middle school."

Payton took the index card from Josie and waved it in the air. "You're always saying you're going to take time off, that you'll put in for a long vacation and see the world—or just hang out here at the farm and do nothing for a while."

"The time for doing nothing is now," announced Josie.

"Yes!" Auntie M clapped her hands together. "You should stay here in the cottage you've fixed up so beautifully. You can sit back and enjoy the holidays, take it easy for once."

"Come on," Payton coaxed. "Stay—at least until the end of the year." Her phone buzzed. She pulled it from the pocket of her floppy cardigan. "It's Easton." Payton's husband would be flying down to join them on Wednesday. "Give me a minute…" Putting the phone to her ear, she moved to the other end of the great room.

Auntie M kept after Alex to spend the holidays at Wild Rose. "You need to relax. Have yourself a real family Thanksgiving and Christmas for once with no pressure to run back to

Portland because of work. Nobody's hiring this time of year anyway. And you just as much as said you're not sure what kind of work you even want yet."

Josie chimed in with, "Take it easy until January. Let the dust settle a little."

"I don't know. Sitting around relaxing sounds vaguely terrifying."

"Because you never let yourself do it," argued Auntie M. "Give yourself a break. You *will* figure it out. But not by rushing into anything. Give your heart and mind time to catch up a little. Your future isn't going anywhere. It will still be there on January first."

"Auntie M knows best," Josie coaxed.

"Yes, I do," said their aunt in a tone both fond and scolding. "So take my advice. No job-hunting till January, at least."

Somehow, the stern expression on her aunt's face made Alex laugh. She admitted, "You know, you're right. All I do is work. I want time off and I'm going to take it." Her stomach felt swoopy just at the thought.

"I'm so glad!" exclaimed Josie as Auntie M beamed in approval.

By then, Payton had finished her call. "Easton says good for you, Alex—and guess what? Easton and my in-laws have ganged up on West."

Weston. Alex ignored the little shiver that slid

beneath her skin at the mention of Easton's identical twin. She'd neither seen nor spoken to West since the first of the year. He hadn't been able to make it for Josie's wedding last spring or for the Fourth of July weekend, either. Nor had he been around the times Alex drove over to visit her sisters and check in on the progress of various improvements she'd arranged at the farm.

Payton went on, "West has been insisting he'll only come down for Christmas, but they've just about convinced him to join us for Thanksgiving, too. He can fly down Wednesday with Easton—there's just one little thing." Payton was looking right at Alex.

Alex got that sinking feeling. "What thing?"

"You may not recall, but I think I mentioned that West came down for a weekend in early August..."

She did remember and she'd stayed in Portland that weekend. "I remember you mentioned he was coming down with Easton, yes."

"That was during the demo phase of the remodel here at the guest cottage, so he stayed in the motor home with Joyce and Myron..." The Wright parents visited the farm often. They brought their own living quarters—a giant luxury motor home with two full en suite bedrooms and every convenience known to man.

Alex felt hope rising. "You're saying Weston will stay in the motor home, then."

"No. I'm saying West *refuses* to stay in the motor home ever again."

"I don't get it. The motor home is gorgeous and climate-controlled, right? It stays cozy no matter how cold it gets outside. And there's plenty of room in there."

Payton wrinkled her nose. "Uh, yeah…no."

"Yeah, no, *what*?"

"You need to understand how Joyce and Myron are—married for decades and still acting like newlyweds. West claims that last summer when he stayed in the motor home with them, he heard things a man should never hear his parents doing."

"Yikes!" Josie snort-laughed.

Payton winced. "Exactly. So this time, West plans to take a suite at the Heartwood Inn." The Wrights owned hotels and resorts up and down the West Coast. They'd bought the Heartwood Inn last year and done a complete renovation. Josie and Miles had been married there in April.

"The inn is beautiful since the renovation," Alex suggested hopefully, though by now she had a pretty good idea of where this conversation was going—and not toward Weston staying at the Heartwood Inn.

"Yes, the inn is gorgeous now," agreed Auntie

M. "But that's not the issue. It's a family weekend and Weston should be with the rest of us, right here on the farm."

They all three stared expectantly at Alex.

And really, why keep stalling? She was bound to come face-to-face with Easton's twin again eventually, though she'd imagined that happening in a more controlled setting—over a family dinner, maybe, during a brief public encounter where they could exchange shallow pleasantries and move on. Not while sharing a small house for a long holiday weekend.

But Auntie M had it right. West was family and they should all be together right here on the farm.

It was only for a few days—and most likely a few more at Christmas. It didn't have to be a big deal if she and West didn't make it one.

Alex gave a firm nod. "Problem solved. I'm happy to share the guest cottage with Weston."

Payton still looked doubtful. "Easton says West feels guilty about moving in on you."

Alex doubted that *guilty* was exactly the word. Uneasy, though? Embarrassed? Self-conscious? All three might apply—they certainly did for her.

"Well, that's just ridiculous," she baldly lied. "It's not as though I need two bedrooms." There was only one bathroom, and they would be sharing it. But no way could she afford to dwell on that right now. "What's the big deal? He's only staying until Sunday, right?"

"Monday, I hope," said Payton. "Kyle and Olga are getting married on Sunday." Alex and her sisters had grown up with Kyle Huckston. His family owned a farm nearby. Kyle's fiancée, Olga Balanchuk, worked at a coffee shop in town. Everybody loved Olga.

Josie said, "The wedding's right here on Wild Rose in the event barn." There were four barns on Wild Rose. A few years ago, Josie and Payton had fixed up one of them for parties, weddings and farm-to-table dinners. Payton and Easton had been married in the event barn last New Year's night, the night Alex got to know West a lot better than she probably should have.

Payton said, "The wedding should be fun, and West likes a nice party..."

"It's no problem."

Did she sound sincere? God, she hoped so. If her sisters or her aunt suspected otherwise, they would keep after her until she told them more than she ever wanted to share of what she'd done with Weston the night of January 1. That couldn't happen. Before they'd parted last winter, she and West had agreed never to share what had happened between them with anyone in either of the families.

Uh-uh. Her sisters and her aunt never needed

to know that she'd spent her sister's wedding night in bed with the groom's brother. "Just tell him I'm happy to share the guest cottage with him."

"Way ahead of you." Payton looked sheepish. "We've been working on West for a while now to get him to stay here at the farm. I already told him I would talk to you and I was sure that you would be fine with him using the back bedroom."

She put on her most sincere expression. "And I am."

"Yeah, but Easton just talked to him a few minutes ago. West is still refusing to budge. He says he doesn't want to impose on you."

"He would not be imposing on me. Reassure him."

"I already did. But maybe if *you* talked to him..."

Terrific. Not only did she have to share a house with him, but she also had to convince him of how much she wanted him there. "Of course. I'll be happy to call him."

"Excellent. You can use my phone." Payton autodialed the number and handed it over so that Alex could convince West right then and there.

He answered on the first ring. "Payton. Hey."

A ridiculous, zingy little thrill skittered through Alex at the sound of his smooth, deep voice. Like she was twelve or something—a preteen with a first crush. "Hi, West. It's, um, Alex.

Payton gave me her phone to call you—because your number is programmed in?"

"Alex..." Long, awful pause. Alex carefully avoided looking at her aunt or either of her sisters. "It's been a minute. How've you been?"

"Great. Fine. Wonderful." Seriously? Three adjectives, each with its own period? *Dial it back, girl. Breathe.* "Payton says you're hesitating to stay here at the guest cottage."

Silence. And then finally, "What? You're surprised?"

She made the mistake of glancing at Payton. Behind Payton, Alex could see Josie on one side and her aunt on the other. All three women were watching her. She put on her best take-charge voice. "There is no need for you to stay at the Heartwood Inn when there's an extra bedroom here at the guest cottage."

"No need, huh? Well, I don't know, Alexandra. The whole point was to avoid each other, wasn't it?" He was razzing her, plain and simple. She could just picture him right now, smirking, his jewel-blue eyes twinkling in his so-handsome, angular face, a face dusted with just the right amount of sexy beard scruff. He and Easton were identical twins, but East was the serious one. West, as a rule, played the lighthearted charmer.

Not last January, though. The night of the wedding, he'd been wrecked over the sudden, completely unexpected loss of his closest friend.

"You won't inconvenience me." Alex tried her best to sound sincere. "There are two bedrooms. You should use one. I mean, that's what they're for, right?" She barreled on, rattling off the reasons he would already have heard from Payton. "It's a family weekend, West. We're all going to be here at the farm. Including you, I hope. Please take the other bedroom."

"Are you sure?"

"Of course. Take the other bedroom. Stay here at the farm with the family."

"Alex?"

"Um, yes?"

"I'm at home at the moment. Alone. Can you talk freely?"

"Yes, well. Payton's right here." She shot a big smile at her youngest sister. "Josie and Auntie M, too. They all say hi."

"Are you on speaker?"

Oh, for heaven's sake. "No, no. Not at all."

"All right, then. Be straight with me."

"I will do my best." *Given the circumstances.*

"We agreed it was a onetime thing and nobody else had to know. You made a big deal in the morning about how we wouldn't contact each other, we'd go right back to being two people who hardly knew each other, the sister of the bride and the brother of the groom." What was he getting at? Pretending nothing had happened really had seemed like the best way to handle things at the time.

And her ears were burning. "Yes. True. That's right. Absolutely."

"*Do* they know?"

She chose her words carefully. "Not from me."

"And not from me."

She breathed a sigh of relief. "I'm so glad to hear that."

"Well then, Alex, I'll need you to tell me honestly. Are you okay with us sharing that little house after what happened last New Year's?"

No, she was not okay with it. And even if they hadn't been each other's one-night stand eleven months ago, she wouldn't really be okay with it.

Because she'd just shocked the hell out of herself and walked out on the job that had been her top priority since she'd finished law school. She needed the cottage all to herself to sit around in her pajamas feeling lost and confused. She needed to stream *Boston Legal* on Hulu, to eat Tillamook Mudslide from the carton as she cried for no real reason while trying to figure out what to do with the rest of her life.

So that was an option, just to say that she needed her alone time and West would intrude on that. Everyone would understand. But then he would stay at the Heartwood Inn and she would feel terrible because that really wasn't right…

And what about just putting the truth out there, just telling everyone that it would be awkward to stay in the cottage with him because she and West had shared a one-night stand? There was nothing unacceptable about what she and West had done. No one here would judge her. Alex and West were both adults, both single. It was nobody's business that they'd had sex on a cold winter night when he'd needed a friend and she was the only one around to hold out a hand. It was one of those things that just happens sometimes.

It would be weird, though, to share that information with the family. Weird and awkward. And Alex still hoped she would never have to go there.

"Alex?" Weston spoke again, his voice so smooth and deep and way too sexy.

"Hmm?"

"You ever plan on answering my question?"

"Absolutely." It came out sounding aggressive, almost angry. She made herself speak more cordially. "Yes. Honestly. There's plenty of room here. You're staying in the cottage. It's settled."

"You're so bossy…" He said that kind of slow—slow and also naughty and she sincerely hoped her cheeks weren't cherry red.

"Weston." She said his name sternly, as a rebuke.

"Alexandra," he mocked.

"That's a yes, right?" Now she made her voice pleasant, even a little too sweet. "You'll take the second bedroom."

"Yes, I will. And it's good to talk to you, Alex. At last." Did he really have to be so…ironic? It wasn't like she hadn't thought more than once of reaching out to him, checking in with him to see how he was holding up. But back in January, when they'd said goodbye, he'd seemed totally on board with cutting it clean. "Alex? You still there?"

"Uh, yes. Great."

"See you day after tomorrow. I'll be flying down with Easton."

"Perfect. See you then." She heard the click as he disconnected the call.

Chapter Two

On Wednesday, West and his brother took an air taxi down to the small airport near Heartwood.

For about half of the short flight, they talked business—together, they ran the family company, Wright Hospitality, East as CEO and West as chief financial officer.

Once they'd moved on from work issues, Easton stared out the window at the clouds for a while. Now and then, he would glance forward. West would get a view of his profile. Easton was grinning, no doubt thinking about his wife, his sons and probably the daughter he would have in mid-January.

East was one of those guys, a family man to the core, a man hopelessly in love his wife. Even during the years he'd lost touch with her, the years he'd had no clue he had twin sons, Easton had carried a torch for Payton—a woman he'd known for a week while scouting the Heartwood Inn in hopes of convincing Wright Hospitality to add the property to their growing list of upscale and midrange hotels and resorts.

Mimicking his twin, West stared at the clouds out his window, too. He was not, nor had he ever been, a family man. He preferred the single life, enjoyed floating on the surface of things, refusing to take anything or anyone too seriously. The thought of getting all wrapped up in one special woman held zero appeal for him.

And yet today, he couldn't stop thinking of Alex, remembering the sound of her voice on the phone the other night. She'd come across as mostly matter-of-fact, yet a little bit nervous. She'd seemed on edge to have to deal with him again, to have him staying in the same house with her for the long weekend.

Just thinking about Alex on edge had him grinning at the white puffs of clouds out the window. In his experience of her up till that phone call, she'd almost always been calm, collected and in control.

Except in bed. In bed, she was all fire. She really let go. They'd only had that one night, but that night stuck with him.

And not only because of the great sex.

It was the night he got the news about Leo. He'd been out of his mind with guilt and grief.

Alex had made that night bearable. She'd been a refuge, a true comfort, a miracle in a world full of pain.

Talking to her again had brought last New Year's night sharply back—both the pain Alex had eased and the pleasure she'd given him. No, he hadn't spent the months since that night thinking about her. She'd definitely crossed his mind, but only now and then. And when he did let himself think of her, he'd felt a certain tug in the vicinity of his heart, something very close to tenderness.

Maybe he shouldn't have teased her on the phone. She'd seemed a little put out at his attitude. But talking to her had kind of gotten to him. He'd felt raw, *known* somehow. Like she really had his number and he needed to watch out, to protect himself from her.

She got under his skin. At the same time, he would always have a soft spot for Alex now. Like a knight riding in on a big white charger—okay, it was an Audi hybrid SUV, but still—Alex had come to his rescue when he'd needed help the most.

Last January 1

By 10:00 p.m. the charming barn wedding was over; the dinner, the toasts, the first dance and the cake-cutting, too. Easton and Payton were now husband and wife.

West's phone buzzed. He pulled it from his pocket and saw he had a voice mail. It was loud in the barn, so he went outside to check the message and return the call.

As soon as he hung up, he grabbed his coat and left the party without saying anything to anyone. He got in his rental car and took off. In the morning, he would reach out to Easton and explain everything.

Halfway to the rented house on the river where he was staying, he started shaking. He had to pull over to the side of the road.

He got out and stood by the driver's door, bent at the waist. A light snow was falling. Shivers racked him and his stomach churned. He had a bad feeling he would chuck his cookies any minute now.

The shock was enormous, the guilt even bigger somehow. He felt he might explode from the power and pain of it. His dearest friend had called him yesterday. West hadn't picked up. It was all about the wedding that day—and today, too. West had planned to reach out to Leo first thing tomorrow.

Too late. He would never be reaching out to Leo again.

A car rolled past, the glare from the headlights sliding over him briefly, then moving on. That happened a few times. He was grateful no one stopped. What would he say if they did?

As he asked himself that question, another pair of headlights flooded over him, pinning him in unwelcome brightness. He heard the crunch of tires on gravel. The light stayed on him. Someone had pulled to the shoulder and stopped right behind his car.

A door opened and shut. Footsteps approached.

Not budging from his crouch, he shouted, "Go away! I'm fine!"

"Weston?" A woman's voice, low-pitched and calm—commanding, even.

He knew that voice. Didn't he? "Alex?"

And then she was right there beside him, Payton's oldest sister, the lawyer from Portland. Her hand touched his back—lightly. Carefully. He got a whiff of her perfume. It was nice, fresh. Not too sweet, almost masculine, really. She asked, "Weston, are you sick?"

He squinted down at dirty snow and her sexy satin high-heeled shoes. "You're going to ruin those shoes," he heard himself say.

"Don't worry about my shoes." Her voice held a hint of humor now.

"What are you doing here?"

"I was heading back to Portland." Of course she was. East had mentioned that the older of Payton's two half sisters was something of a workaholic, that Alex never stayed at Wild Rose Farm for more than a day or two at a stretch.

"Weston. Can you walk?"

Still bent over, staring at the ground, he groaned. "I really don't want to talk right now."

"And you don't have to." She took his arm. "Come on. I'll drive you."

"Where?"

"Anywhere you want to go."

"Really, I'm okay."

"This way." Her voice was so comforting all of a sudden. Like a pillow. Like something soft that you could also depend on. Gently, she guided him upright.

He shook his head. "The car…"

"It will be fine here for a while."

He just didn't feel like arguing with her. "All right. Have it your way. Let me get the keys."

She released his arm and stepped back, those satin shoes crunching gravel. He grabbed the door latch, yanked it open—and remembered that the key was in his pocket. The car had remote start.

Shutting the door again, he beeped the locks.

She claimed his arm once more. He let her lead him to her Audi. When she opened the door for him, he slid obediently into the passenger seat and buckled right up.

"Where to?" she asked once she'd settled in behind the wheel.

He gave her directions to the house on the river. The short drive passed in silence.

"Thanks for the ride," he said when she stopped the car in the driveway. "I've got my keys. I'll be fine."

She refused to take the hint. Instead, she pushed open her door, swung her legs out and stood. Apparently, she was going inside with him. He didn't have the energy to insist that she leave, so he said nothing. The path to the front door had been shoveled clear of snow. They went up the front steps together. She followed him in.

The house had an open plan. It was all windows on the river side, with wraparound decks in a sort of rustic contemporary style. They hung their coats in the mudroom area off the entry.

In the great room, she asked, "You want a drink or something? Maybe coffee?" Like she was the one staying here, not him.

He stood by the leather sofa and stared past the dining area table and beyond it at the gleaming stainless-steel appliances, the subway tile backsplashes and quartz counters. "No liquor," he said. "Not now. And I'm not up for making coffee."

"It's fine." She grabbed one of the two remotes from the low sofa table and pointed it at the fireplace. Flames licked up. He blinked at her in wonder. How could she know that remote worked the fireplace? She was like a general, masterful. Confident. Not one foot soldier would be lost under her command. "Sit down, Weston. I'll make the coffee."

He did as she instructed, turning and dropping to the sofa. For a while, he stared out the window at a section of snow-covered deck. He listened to the soft sound of the river rushing by out there in the dark and smelled coffee brewing.

Eventually, she set a tray on the low table and took one of the chairs across from him. "Cream and sugar?"

"Black."

She filled them each a mug and took a chocolate chip biscotti from the pretty pottery dish next to the carafe. He hadn't even known there was biscotti. The house was Easton's, rented when he first returned to Oregon back in October.

"Drink your coffee," she instructed.

He picked up the mug and had a sip. It went down all right, so he had another. It helped, to have something to do, to feel the warmth of the mug between his hands.

Alex crossed her long, smooth legs and leaned forward in the chair. "Talk to me, Weston."

He opened his mouth to tell her to mind her own damn business. Instead, he heard himself mutter, "My best friend, Leo, died today. His mother called to let me know."

She uncrossed those great legs of hers and leaned in closer. He waited for her to say something sympathetic. Then he would sneer at her, let her know she had no idea what he might be feeling right now.

But she didn't say a word. She simply waited, watching him.

And he started talking about Leo, about how they met when they were assigned as roommates in the dorms freshman year at UCLA.

Right away, they'd hit it off, West and Leo. Leo was smart and fun and bighearted, the life of the party—until he wasn't. Leo had mood swings. He'd been diagnosed with bipolar disorder in his senior year of high school.

Over their four years at UCLA, Leo and West had developed a bond, a deep bond, one that had held strong even after West moved back to Seattle eight years ago to take his place at Wright Hospitality. "I was best man at his wedding," West said. "Leo was the happiest guy in the world that day…"

But the marriage only lasted four years. "He

started spiraling more often after his marriage broke up. Still, we stayed close, stayed in touch. We managed to get together a few times a year, at least. It hasn't been the same, though."

"How so?"

"With Leo in Los Angeles and me in Seattle, we haven't been able to hang out a couple of times a week the way we used to. Sometimes Leo complains..." West hung his head. "I mean, *complained*. Because Leo will never complain again, will he?" He sent her a belligerent glance.

Her eyes held only understanding. "No, Weston. He won't."

His throat felt so dry. He sipped more coffee. "Where was I?"

"You said that sometimes Leo complained—"

"Right. He always said things were so much better when I was still working in LA. He said once that he wished *he* had a twin. Leo's my best friend, but with East, it's deeper. And in the family, East has always been the solid one, the both-feet-on-the-ground one. In the family, I always felt like the lightweight, you know? East always had all the answers. With Leo, though, it's the other way around. With Leo, I'm—I *was* the strong one, the one Leo could count on."

They sat in silence for a moment. It felt so natural. Like he'd known her forever, long enough to be quiet with her and not feel strange about it.

She asked how Leo had died.

He said, "Hiking Mount Baldy in the San Gabriel Mountains. He was with his cousin Ray. Ray's a great guy, with a nice wife and two kids. There were frozen spots on the trail. Leo's mom said it was just an accident, that they were joking around together and they slipped on a patch of ice—both of them. They slid more than a hundred feet straight down. Ray got bumps and bruises. But Leo hit his head somehow. He died instantly…"

"I'm so sorry, Weston." She said it softly.

"I keep thinking that maybe it wasn't an accident. That Leo needed me. And I wasn't there and he decided he couldn't keep going anymore…"

"You just said he wasn't alone, that someone trustworthy was with him, someone who slipped and fell when he did."

"Yeah, but how will I ever know for sure?"

She held his gaze. "Life's hard enough. Don't make it harder."

"Alex, he called me yesterday. I kept meaning to call back…"

"Weston, don't start blaming yourself."

"Just call me West."

She continued to hold him with those knowing eyes of hers. He couldn't look away. "It's not your fault."

He set his mug on the tray. "I have to go down there, to LA tomorrow—and okay, you've got a point. His mom seemed really certain he wasn't depressed, that the fall was purely accidental. I just wish I'd called him back."

"It was your brother's wedding day. You had a lot going on."

"It's no excuse."

"Stop. There was no way you could have known what would happen."

"I want to believe you so bad." Now, all of a sudden, he couldn't face her. He braced his elbows on his knees and put his head in his hands. "But I don't believe you."

She got up, circled the low table and sat beside him. Her clean, soothing scent came to him again.

He let her take his hand. Her long, smooth fingers felt just right wrapped in his. He realized he was glad she'd stuck with him, grateful that she hadn't let him send her on her way.

"I changed my mind," he said, still holding tight to her hand. "I don't want to be alone tonight."

"I know," she answered quietly, stating a simple fact. "You shouldn't be alone."

"If it were any other night I would've gone

straight to Easton." He shook his head. "I couldn't do that to him, though, not on his wedding night. So you kind of got stuck with me."

"See? You're a good brother. Just like it's very clear you were a great friend to Leo. And I'm not 'stuck' with you. I want to be here. I feel *right* about being here. Sometimes you just need someone. I hope, for tonight, you'll let that someone be me."

He was looking deep in those sable-brown eyes of hers again, thinking that really, he hardly knew her. He'd met her for the first time the day before when she drove over from Portland for the wedding rehearsal. Initially, he'd found her smart, career-focused, good-looking and kind of cold. A bit distant.

But now he saw how unfair his initial impression had been. She was amazing, so patient and strong. Unruffled. A lifeline in a world gone horribly wrong.

"Thank you," he said. "For not leaving me alone." And then he was leaning closer, magnetized—to her. To the comfort and understanding she offered.

A small gasp of surprise escaped her when she realized that he would kiss her. He half expected her to push him away. She probably *should* push him away.

But she didn't. She melted into him.

Her mouth was so soft. He sank into the kiss, wrapping his arms around her, pulling her closer.

In his room a little later, they agreed on that night—one night and that would be all. He wasn't looking for more and neither was she. Nobody in the families ever had to know.

She warned, "You know we're going to have to sit across from each other at family dinners for the rest of our lives. You think you're up for that?"

God, he wanted her by then. She'd made this night survivable for him. She was a beckoning golden light in a sea of darkness. He needed to get lost in her, at least for a while.

"I've got no problem with seeing you across the table when the family gets together. I want this, you and me, Alex. Just for tonight—but not if you don't. You need to tell me if you've changed your mind."

She laughed then, the sound husky and warm. "I haven't changed my mind. You said I was helping you."

"And you are. You have no idea how much."

"Well, you're helping me, too. I've never done anything like this before—never had just one night with a man, a night to let go, a night just to feel. I seriously doubt that I'll ever do it again. But this seems right."

"For me, too. So right."

"And, West, I can handle the family dinners. I promise you."

He stared at her mouth and couldn't wait to kiss her again. "All right, then?"

She nodded. "We understand each other."

He reached for her and they fell across the bed together.

She tasted so good. The rest of the world vanished. It didn't even exist. It was only the two of them, West and Alex. For a while, she was everything, and nothing else mattered. He didn't think about what would happen tomorrow, about the best friend he'd lost, the friend he would never see again. There was only Alex, soft and sleek and sighing, on fire in his arms.

Nothing else, only her—and he was found instead of lost all through the darkest part of the night.

In the morning early, she drove him to his rental car. They said goodbye. He stood there at the side of the road, hands stuffed in the pockets of his heavy winter jacket, watching her drive away.

Out the window of the small plane, the clouds had thinned to pale wisps. West hadn't seen Alex since she dropped him off at his car that morning after Easton's wedding.

But he would see her now.

"What are you grinning about?" Easton was watching him.

West met those blue eyes identical to his own. "Hey, I get a big turkey dinner and I'm not staying in the motor home. Life is good."

A few minutes later, they landed at the small airport not far from Heartwood where they each had a rental car waiting. A half an hour after that, West stood on the porch of Payton's cottage hugging first his mom and then his dad. His parents had arrived a couple of hours earlier. He greeted Payton and his nephews.

Penn and Bailey loved the farm. They wanted to do everything at once—ride the ponies their doting grandfather had bought them last year, go get a Christmas tree before Thanksgiving had even happened. They wanted snow, please. Right now. So they could build a snowman.

"Sorry, guys. Did you notice? No snow yet," Easton said patiently.

"And you already rode the ponies once today," Payton reminded them.

"Please, Mom," wheedled Bailey. West could have sworn the two boys had each grown an inch since the last time he saw them a couple of weeks ago.

"One more ride..." Penn piled on the pressure.

Their desperate pleading had the desired effect on the doting grandparents. West's dad leaned close to Easton and whispered something.

East nodded. "Sure, if you want to."

"Okay, you two," said Myron. "Another ride it is. Put on your jackets."

The boys ran inside and came right back out.

"We're ready!" crowed Bailey. He grabbed his grandma's hand and Penn took Grandpa's. Off the four of them went to tack up the ponies and give the boys a ride around the horse pasture.

About then, Marilyn and Ernesto emerged from Marilyn's cottage across the way. The two stopped to chat with the boys and the grandparents.

Beside him on the porch, East and Payton were whispering together, pausing for a kiss—and then whispering some more. They were as bad as the grandparents, constantly canoodling. East bent to kiss his wife's enormous belly and West glanced away just as the door to the next cottage over swung inward.

Alex emerged in a bulky red sweater, jeans and sturdy boots. She looked great. Determined and focused as ever, ready to take on the world and bend it to her will. He might have gotten half-hard, just seeing her again. In her floppy sweater and tan boots, she looked good, more relaxed than last January.

He watched as she greeted his mom and dad.

The group broke up, the grandparents and boys moving on toward the barns, Ernesto, Marilyn and Alex coming this way.

A moment later, Alex was mounting the steps. He looked in those big brown eyes and she gave him a little smile. "West, how have you been?"

"Can't complain. You?"

"Taking it easy." She had her coffee-brown hair pulled back in a low ponytail. It was a little longer than last January. He remembered how thick it was, warm and silky against his skin as he wrapped a big hank of it slowly around his hand…

Down, boy. Everyone would know how glad he was to see her if he didn't keep a tight rein on certain memories of that night.

Still, he really wanted to step in nice and close to her, to breathe in that perfume he'd liked so much, maybe give her ponytail a tug.

"Come on inside, everyone." Payton pushed open the door to her cottage.

They all filed in. East carried his suitcases into the downstairs bedroom. Payton offered coffee.

Alex asked, "West, do you want to unpack first?" Her voice betrayed nothing. She was a cool one, the kind of woman who keeps a man on his toes.

"Good idea." He shared quick greetings with

Marilyn and Ernesto and then followed Alex out. "I'll just drive my car over."

"There's a parking space next to my Audi on the far side of the house."

"Got it. Want a ride?"

She shook her head. "See you in a minute." And off she went along the well-tended dirt road that ran in a circle between the cottages.

When he carried his suitcase and laptop up the steps, she was waiting for him, holding open the door.

He entered the great room. It was looking good, with a sofa and chairs grouped around a coffee table on one side, a gas fireplace on the other. A door on the sofa side led back to a small hallway. The sparkling new kitchen area was straight ahead.

"It looks terrific," he said, and meant it. The floor was dark hardwood with a tan rug under the furniture. The fire licked up through crystals and driftwood behind a glass screen. She had a modern jewel-blue sofa and two comfy-looking leather club chairs.

"Yeah, it came out really nice, I think—come on. Your room is this way."

She led him into the small square of hallway, sweeping out a hand at the bathroom as they passed it. "We're sharing the bathroom." It was basic—a tub and shower combo, a toilet, a sink.

The tub tile was vivid turquoise and so was the wall behind the sink.

"It's pretty," he said.

She nodded. "And small. Your room is here."

It was kind of a tight fit in the little hallway. As he eased past her, he got a whiff of her scent. Clean and serene, just as he remembered.

The back bedroom was cozy, all right. The platform bed took up most of the floor space. There was a dresser and a tiny closet. The window looked out on a stretch of garden. In the distance, he could see a red barn and an orchard, a few orange and red leaves still clinging to the trees.

He swung his suitcase onto the bed and set his laptop on the dresser. "Thanks for putting me up."

"Happy to."

He wanted to call her a liar, but that would be just asking for trouble—which he was pretty much bound to do eventually. But no need to get up in her face right off the bat. "You know how they are—your family and mine both."

She leaned in the doorway, folded her arms across her middle and declared in a syrupy tone, "It's a family holiday. And we all need to be together at the farm."

"You'd never guess that a year ago, Payton wasn't speaking to my parents, Easton was scared to death he would never get her to marry him, and you and I hadn't even met..."

Her eyes had a distant look in them now. "Hey. A lot can happen in a year."

He offered honestly, "Alex, I was really sorry to hear about your dad."

She glanced away and then back. Those big eyes were sad now. "We weren't close. But thank you—and what about your trip to LA? I did wonder how you were doing down there, how you were getting through it all..."

"It was tough."

"I'm so sorry."

"But there were good moments. I had some time with Leo's mom and dad. I felt better after I talked to them. You know I had my doubts about the accident..."

Her reply was somber. "You wondered if it really was an accident."

He nodded. "Yeah. That. But I saw his cousin Ray—the guy who was with him when it happened?"

"I remember you mentioned Ray, yes."

"Ray and me, we talked a little. Ray said what Leo's mom said. That it was an accident, pure and simple. He and Leo were exhausted from the hike up the mountain, but they were having a great time, razzing each other about how they were getting old, getting soft—just, you know, doing what guys do. Ray said they were both laughing when it happened."

Now her eyes had the sheen of unshed tears. She blinked the moisture away. "It's so sad to lose your friend."

"Yeah. I miss him. Leo could be really funny. And he was generous. He was always lending people money and half the time they never paid him back. At the funeral, people got up and said true things about him—good things. They played all his favorite music. He liked those ancient disco bands. The Bee Gees and ABBA. He had a major crush on Donna Summer. As funerals go, it was great."

"I'm glad that there were good moments." Her voice was husky, whisper-soft.

"There were, yeah. Real good."

For several seconds, they just stared at each other. Every word, every touch, every sigh from that night all those months ago seemed to hang in the air between them.

Then she straightened from the doorway. "Listen, I should let you get settled in."

"Yeah. Sounds like a plan." He made his voice brisk, like he couldn't wait to start emptying his suitcase. For a minute or two there, he'd had that feeling about her, same as last year. Like they were really close. Like he could tell her anything and she would listen, she would understand.

But they did have an agreement. What had happened at the house on the river stayed at the house on the river. Right now, they were relatives by marriage and Thanksgiving roommates, no more.

"I shopped for groceries yesterday," she said. "The fridge and pantry are fully stocked. Help yourself to anything you're hungry for…"

"Will do. Thanks, Alex."

When she turned and disappeared into the living area, he wanted to trot along right behind her. But he didn't. He knew the rules and he fully intended to stick by them.

Chapter Three

"Come on, you guys! Let's play go fish!" hollered Bailey, waving a deck of cards.

Alex just happened to be sitting next to him. He'd shouted the words directly into her ear. She winced at his caterwauling—and then grabbed him. As she gave him a noogie, she reminded him, "Who forgot to use his inside voice?"

"Aunt Alex, stop! No! Let me go..." He dissolved into giggles.

She planted a kiss on the side of his head before releasing him. "No more yelling in my ear, or I might just have to do that again."

It was after dinner that night. They were all sitting around the great room in the big Craftsman-style house on Halstead Farm, where Josie lived with her husband, Miles, and their blended family.

"Go fish, you guys!" shouted Penn. "Come on, me and Bailey want to play."

"Keep it down, son," Easton chided gently just as Davy, Josie's boy, who was almost ten months old, started crying. Maybe from all the yelling by the twins—or maybe because he was teething.

"I think he's wet," declared Miles's fourteen-year-daughter, Hazel, in whose lap the baby was sitting. "I'll change him." She got up, hoisted Davy to her shoulder and headed for his room.

The twins settled cross-legged on the floor at the big coffee table. Penn demanded, "Come on, Mom. Play with us."

"Can't." Payton patted her giant belly. "Baby bump privileges. If I get down on that floor, I may never get up."

Bailey chortled at that as Penn turned pleading eyes on Alex. "Aunt Alex? Please?"

She had a serious food baby of her own, but she was putty in the hands of both of those boys. Alex slid to the floor next to Bailey as Penn continued to make puppy-dog eyes at all the adults.

Wouldn't you know, West settled in cross-legged right next to her. "I'll play." He slid her a glance he probably meant to seem innocent. Too bad there was nothing the least bit innocent about Weston Wright.

"Such fun," she said drily.

He leaned closer. He smelled good, as she remembered all too well—clean and woodsy with a hint of spice. "Watch out. I'm dangerous at go fish."

She snickered. "I think you're just dangerous, period." It took her a few seconds to realize they were staring at each other.

Quickly, she looked away as Miles and his gorgeous older daughter, seventeen-year-old Ashley, joined them around the low table.

Through four games of go fish, Alex took special care not to share any lingering glances with the hot guy to her left. How was it that trying not to look at him only made her want to look at him more?

Still, the game was fun. The boys were in their element, laughing a lot, bossing each other around. Josie and Donna, Miles's mom, served coffee and hot cider. The homey great room was full of the people Alex loved the most, everyone either arguing over the game or making plans, coordinating the big turkey dinner at Auntie M's tomorrow night. Miles's border collie, Bruce, and Tinkerbell, Josie's Dutch shepherd, were stretched out by the fire side by side while Hazel's calico cat, Miss Edith, sat in the arch to the front hall, her fluffy tail wrapped neatly around her pretty white paws.

The group thinned out around eight thirty. Payton and East took the boys home to bed. Ashley's handsome boyfriend, Chase, arrived to take Ash to a party. Miles's mom left for her house in town. And then Auntie M and Ernesto called it a night. Alex had ridden over there with them, but the guest cottage was less than a mile from the Halsteads' house. She hugged her aunt goodbye and said she would walk home.

Weston, who had come over with Easton, Payton and the boys, said, "Alex, wait up. I'm heading back, too."

So they walked together, hands stuffed in the pockets of their winter jackets, ice crunching under their boots, collars turned up. Mostly, they were silent. Overhead, a pale sliver of new moon peeked in and out through the clouds. Once, she glanced his way just as he looked over at her. His nose was red. Hers must be, too. Their breath came out as mist.

He gave her a crooked, totally charming smile. "Good dinner."

"Excellent," she agreed, and tried not to think about how it might feel to kiss him right now—how their lips would be so cold at first, quickly growing warm, how they might pull back a little to grin at each other when their frozen noses bumped together…

At the guest cottage, she insisted that he use the bathroom first. He was quick, disappearing into his room for the night not ten minutes later. She had a shower, brushed her teeth and corralled her still-damp hair into Dutch braids.

When she climbed into bed, sleep didn't come. She felt energized—and edgy, too. As though a current buzzed just beneath the surface of her skin. She kept thinking of West in the other room. He was probably sleeping like a baby by now, without a care in the world.

She, on the other hand…

Her life was all up in the air. She didn't even know if she wanted to live in Portland anymore. Probably, yes. It was the biggest city in Oregon and not that far from home. And she would need to do something constructive with her life, even if she did happen to be ridiculously wealthy now. She really ought to do something with her years of experience in corporate law. Maybe she could set up her own practice, do a lot of pro bono work, try to give back somehow. Or create a foundation of some kind, help out women who were struggling to bring in a paycheck and raise their children, too.

It all felt kind of overwhelming. Her father had never been there for her when he was alive.

Now, in death, he had thoroughly messed with her life plan.

She sat up, punched her pillow and flopped back down, disgusted with herself. Oh, she had it so rough, now didn't she? She was single, with no children, free to go wherever she wanted, do whatever she pleased. And she had more money than she knew what to do with.

Poor, poor Alex…

"Tea," she whispered to herself, shoving the covers back, swinging her feet to the rug and reaching for her big, comfy cardigan. Valerian tea would relax her, help her stop freaking out about things that really weren't even a problem. In no time, she would be drifting off to sleep.

Wide-awake in the back bedroom, West was thinking about Alex—and he shouldn't be. But somehow, he couldn't stop.

He wasn't supposed to—he'd promised himself not to. And yet, after all these months, he still wanted to jump her. Sexually speaking, she had that certain something. She did it for him, riled him up but good.

He'd never met a woman so hot and yet simultaneously so smooth, so in control. He wanted to heat her up, shred that control to tatters.

But no.

They'd agreed not to go there.

He needed to hold up his end of their deal.

When she was cool, he needed to be cooler. He needed *not* to want her so much harder than she could *not* want him.

It was keeping him awake, all this thinking about not wanting her.

Maybe some hot milk would settle him down—or better yet, a glass of scotch.

He got up, pulled on sweatpants and a sweatshirt and went looking for something relaxing to drink.

Instead, he found Alex in a giant sweater and flannel pajama pants, with her hair in braids like a Disney heroine. She sat on a stool at the kitchen island, resting her chin in one hand and dipping a tea bag into a mug with the other.

"What's that you're drinking?"

She gave him one of those so-patient looks of hers. "Sleepyhead Tea. It's got valerian."

"Who?"

"Valerian. It's an herb. Helps you sleep."

"Does it work?" He took the stool beside her.

"Yeah. Want some?" She pushed the mug and saucer over in front of him. "All yours. I'll brew myself another." She jumped up, rounded the island and got down a mug, a saucer and a tea bag.

He carefully removed the tea bag from the mug she'd given him. "Is it good?"

"It helps you sleep." She poured water from

an electric kettle over the fresh tea bag. "It's not about the flavor."

"Scotch helps you sleep. It tastes great."

"Factually speaking, scotch does not help you sleep—or if it does, once the buzz fades, you're likely to wake up."

"Okay, okay. I'll try the tea." It really didn't smell all that fantastic. But he sipped it anyway.

"Well?"

He sipped again. "Hmm. Kind of funky, with subtle notes of gym socks."

She laughed. He liked her laugh a lot. It was husky and real. "All right, West. I'll get the scotch for you."

"Never mind."

"You sure?"

He nodded. "The tea is fine."

She brought her own mug over and sat beside him again. "What are you doing up?"

"Just couldn't sleep." Okay, it was a partial lie. So what? She didn't need to know that thinking about boning her again was giving him insomnia. "You?"

She puffed out her cheeks with a hard breath. "Life. Jobs. What to do next. All that..."

He sipped more funky tea and tried not to remember the most intimate things—the velvety feel of her skin, the taste of her, the sounds she made. “Easton told me you decided to leave your job in Portland.”

“Yeah. The truth is, I don’t need that job anymore. I never have to work again. My dad left me more money than I know what to do with.”

“And having a lot of money is a problem somehow?”

She flipped one of her braids back over her shoulder. “It’s a very long story.”

“I’m listening. And I like those braids.” He really wanted to pull on one.

“Thank you.”

“You seem pissed off at your dad.”

She stared into her tea. “Yeah. I guess I am—scratch that. I *know* I am.”

What was it about being alone with someone in the middle of the night that made them get honest, made them admit things they might not say in the harsh light of day?

Tonight, that seemed to be the case with Alex. “My dad loved my mother,” she said. “Too bad for him, my mother only loved herself. She dumped him for a teenage soldier, Josie’s dad, who died when Josie was a baby.”

“East told me about Payton’s dad, that Payton never met the guy.”

“That’s right. The identity of Payton’s dad remains a mystery. My mother’s love life was wide-ranging. She never really settled down with one guy. She died when I was fourteen. By then, all three of us—Payton, Josie and me—knew not to depend on her for anything. All three of us were raised here on the farm. But I lived in a big house in Portland's West Hills for the first year and a half of my life—not that I remember living there. When my mom, Adrienne, dumped my dad, she dropped me off with Auntie M here at Wild Rose. Josie and Payton were born here. Adrienne would come back to the farm whenever she needed a place to stay. Auntie M was our mother in all the ways that count."

He suggested gently, "But back to your dad…"

She shrugged. "When my mother divorced him, my dad moved to Southern California. He had no more time for me than my mother did."

"But you had your aunt."

"Exactly. She was all the mother we needed, my sisters and me."

"Did your dad have other kids?"

"Nope. And he never got married again as far as anyone knows. What he did do was make money in real estate. A lot of money. At one time, he owned his own real estate business, Herrera Group, with offices in LA, Palm Springs, San Francisco and Seattle. But then a few years ago, he sold the business and retired. He played golf a lot. Died on the golf course, as a matter of fact.

"To give credit where credit is due, he did

pay child support until I was eighteen—too bad that, until my mother died, he wrote the checks to her. She took the money and spent it on God knows what. I rarely saw her or my dad. She only showed up when she needed something and he never asked for visitation. But at least he sent the checks to Aunt Marilyn once my mom was gone. That money helped out a lot."

"Tell me he helped you with college, at least."

"Sorry, but no. One of the few times he showed up in Oregon to see me, he explained that it would be character-building for me to pay for my own education."

"So you put yourself through college?"

"I had some scholarships, but not a full ride. I've spent my life counting only on myself, my sisters and Auntie M—and then what happens? My dad dies and leaves me a fortune."

He wanted to put an arm around her, hold her close. But he knew she wouldn't go for that. "I can see why you're pissed off. Money's nice. But your dad should have been there for you."

"Yeah. I wanted my dad. I couldn't see why he didn't want me back. And then eventually I accepted reality and moved on." She gave him a crooked little smile followed by that wonderful, husky laugh. "The irony is I've been scrimping and saving for most of my life. I've worked killer hours at the firm so I would be ready if the farm ever got in trouble, or if Josie or Payton got in a jam. Now I find out I could have taken it easy because dear old Dad ended up leaving everything to me."

Though he knew he probably shouldn't, West leaned a little closer to her. She smelled so good. He imagined pressing his lips to the soft skin of her throat. "Let's focus on the bright side here."

"You're right. I'm rich. I should be happier about it. I actually feel kind of guilty that I'm *not* happier about it."

He couldn't help laughing when she said that.

She bopped him on the arm with the back of her hand. "West. It's not funny."

"Yeah, it kind of is. Lighten up."

She shifted sideways just enough that her shoulder brushed his arm. He wished she would do that again. "I can't lighten up." She put on an exaggerated sulky face and whined, "Not yet. I think I'm in shock. I still can't believe I walked out on my job."

"Do you think you made a mistake, walking out?"

"No. It's not that. I know I made the right choice. The reason for my working at Kauffman, Judd and Tisdale no longer applies. I was there for the money, pure and simple. It wasn't cool to just walk out like that, but I needed to quit."

"And you could afford to walk out. You just surprised yourself. Nothing wrong with that."

She peered at him through narrowed eyes and accused, "You're very insightful, West, you know that?"

"Are you saying I don't seem like the insightful type?"

"No, not at all. It was only an observation."

"Alex, there's more for you to be happy about than just the fortune you've inherited."

"Hit me with it. Please."

"With your corporate law background, you know how to manage the money your dad left you."

"Yes, I do."

"Would you have gone to law school if you'd always known your dad planned to leave everything to you?"

"Maybe not. All my life, I've been driven to look out for the family, to be ready if they need me, to earn enough money that I can stave off potential disaster."

"So then, look at it this way. Though you didn't know it at the time, you were always preparing yourself to manage the money your father would leave to you. If you *had* known you were your dad's only heir, it could have gone differently and not in a good way."

"You mean I could have been a slacker?"

"No way. I can't see you as a slacker under any

circumstances. But you might have chosen a different career path and then ended up with no idea what to do with the money you would eventually inherit."

"West. I've hired investment managers. I could have done that even without a background in law."

"But could you have hired them knowledgeably?"

She slapped a hand on the granite countertop. "What do you know? I'm knee-deep in silver linings. I know how to manage my inheritance—and what about this cottage?"

He teased, "Are you changing the subject?"

"No. I'm counting my silver linings. I fixed this cottage up with my dad's money and I love how it turned out. It's small, but cozy."

"Yes, it is."

"Josie, Payton and I talked about expanding the footprint of the house, but we decided against it. It's perfect as a guest house. And a couple of months ago, also with the money my dad left me, I set up trust funds for all three of my nephews. As soon as my niece is born, I'll set up one for her."

"Spreading the wealth. Admirable."

"And then I thought about Ash and Hazel…"

"Hold on. You lost me."

"Josie's stepdaughters."

"Okay…"

"I thought, why leave them out? Miles wasn't on board at first. He seemed to think that would somehow be taking advantage of me and he wanted to make it clear that he was on the job as a dad, that he'd saved for their educations, that he could afford to back them up in whatever they wanted to do in life."

West had no doubt how that had worked out. "You changed his mind."

"He took some convincing, but in the end, he gave me his blessing. So I set up trust funds for the girls, too—not that any of my nieces and nephews are going to end up in need. Payton just signed another seven-figure book deal and you know how well your brother is doing. And as I already said, Josie and Miles are doing fine, too."

"*You're* going to be fine. Wait and see."

Her shoulders drooped. "It's just that, suddenly, I hardly know myself. I mean, I've always been a planner. And now I'm realizing that my plans have gotten me exactly nowhere. I'm still leasing an apartment because of my plans, which included waiting to buy a house until I made partner and funded my buy-in. I had it all laid out for myself, how my life would go. And then Monday, I had Chinese for lunch."

"Hold on. You lost me there. What does Chinese food have to do with anything?"

"I'm saying, I took one look at the fortune in my cookie and quit my job." She got up, grabbed an index card from under a magnet on the refrigerator and handed it to him across the island.

He read, *"Do it now."*

"That's me, West."

"Doing it now?" He didn't mean to sound hopeful, but it might have come out that way.

Folding her arms under her breasts, which he couldn't help wishing he might see again someday, she announced, "What I mean is, I have *all* the big plans. And yet, I quit my job because of a fortune cookie—and all my big plans came to nothing."

"Come back here." He patted the empty stool beside him.

She yawned. "I think the tea might be working."

Really, he was having far too good a time to let her run off to her room right now. He patted her stool again.

Surprised the hell out of him when she marched back around the island and hopped up beside him. "Now I just need to figure out what to do with the rest of my life."

"Cut yourself some slack. Relax a little. You'll get there."

"Maybe I'll go to a sperm bank and have a baby, like Josie did with Davy. Or maybe I'll adopt.

There are a lot of kids out there who need mothers, you know? Even a disgruntled single career woman for a mother is better than no mother at all."

"I don't see you as disgruntled." He saw her as hot—and, tonight at least, way too damn hard on herself.

She made the cutest little pouty face. "Well, I certainly do feel disgruntled."

"Maybe get a puppy first—before signing on for a baby, I mean."

She braced her elbow on the counter and her head on her hand. They stared at each other. He would only have to lean in a few inches to kiss her—but he wasn't going to do that. As he constantly reminded himself, they'd agreed on that one night and no more. "You might be right about the puppy," she said. "I've always wanted a dog, but with my work schedule, it just made no sense..."

"See? More silver linings. You have no work schedule at the moment. You can finally adopt a puppy."

With two fingers, she pushed her empty mug and saucer toward the other side of the island. "Thank you."

"For what?"

"For listening." A little sigh escaped her. "For saying all the right things."

"You did the same for me not that long ago."

Her eyes were low, lazy. He felt pretty relaxed himself. The funky tea must be working.

Those lips of hers…

He really wanted to taste them again, wanted to ease a hand under those Disney braids to clasp the back of her neck. He wanted to pull her to him, right up close.

Pull her to him, kiss her for a long time and then scoop her up and carry her to the back bedroom. She made him feel…open, somehow.

Like she saw right down inside him and accepted what she saw.

He liked her. Too much.

And he wanted her.

A lot.

And maybe, over the months since last New Year's, he'd thought about her more often than he'd let himself admit.

Really, he needed to watch himself with her. Get a grip. Behave.

They had an agreement and it wouldn't be a good idea to mess with it. Last January, she'd made it crystal clear where she stood—and so had he.

If they got something going, there was way too big a chance it wouldn't end well. He wasn't his parents or his brother. He was missing the true-love-forever gene.

But what about her? Alex seemed no more interested in romance than he was.

And that had him thinking that maybe they could reach another agreement, just for the holiday weekend—and possibly for Christmas, too…

No. Uh-uh. Terrible idea. There were far too many ways a plan like that could go wrong.

His stool scraped the floor as he jumped to his feet. "It's getting really late."

Alex sat up straighter. For a split second, he thought he'd upset her. But then her soft lips curved in a lazy smile. "Good night, West."

"Night." He turned and left her there before he did something he would only end up regretting.

Alex waited until she heard the door to the back bedroom click shut before she carried the mugs and saucers to the sink and loaded them into the dishwasher. She took a minute to empty the electric kettle and wipe down the island.

Then she headed for her own room.

Once she'd shut and locked the door, she let her head fall back and—very quietly—groaned at the ceiling.

West Wright was dangerous. He was too sexy, too charming. Very intelligent. And altogether too perceptive.

She *liked* him, damn it. Too much. He just… well, he got to her in a very good way. West made her laugh and he spoke to her honestly. She could feel the heat between them. She knew he was trying just as hard as she was not to do anything they might both regret. It would be beyond stupid to fall into bed with him again—and he knew that as well as she did.

When it came to her and West, the last thing they needed was to *Do it now.*

Chapter Four

"West? You awake?" It was Alex's voice. Three gentle taps on the door came next.

West cracked an eye open. Bright sunshine slipped in through the narrow spaces between the shut blinds. He grabbed his phone off the little table by the bed to check the time: 8:05—and he had a couple of texts from his brother, the first one from a half an hour before.

Breakfast at our cottage. Mom's making patty cakes.

West's stomach growled. He loved patty cakes, which were also called German pancakes, hootenannies and Dutch baby pancakes. Whatever you called them, they were light and fluffy and absolutely delicious.

And five minutes ago, East had texted: West. Mom says breakfast. Now.

More tapping on the bedroom door. "West?"

"Yeah, Alex. I'm awake!"

"Breakfast at Payton's. We're supposed to be there now. Your mom's cooking. I'm going on over."

"Okay. See you there." He tapped out a response to East: On my way…

Five minutes later, he pulled on his jacket and went out the door. The sun was shining, but damn, was it cold. He zipped up his coat and hunched into the wind for the short walk to the next cottage over.

Penn pulled open the door. "It's Uncle Weston!" he bellowed.

East appeared behind his son. "'Bout time. Get in here before we all freeze to death."

The small house was wall-to-wall family. People sat wherever they could find a space, some of them balancing their full plates on their knees.

His mother stood at the kitchen counter making her special oven-raised pancakes in shifts. She was pink-cheeked and smiling, in her element, cooking breakfast for a crowd. He'd never seen her as happy as she'd been since Easton married Payton. At last his mom had grandsons to spoil and a granddaughter on the way. She and his dad had grown up on neighboring ranches about forty miles east of Seattle. They both loved Wild Rose. For them, the farm was like coming home. Every chance they got, they would pack up their motor home and head down to Oregon.

West hung his jacket over another coat on one of the overburdened pegs by the door. East handed him a full mug of coffee. A few minutes later another batch of patty cakes emerged from the oven, smelling of eggs, flour and sugar, reminding him of his childhood. His mom buttered him up a serving, dusted it with powdered sugar and gave him the maple syrup so he could drizzle it on top.

"Sausage?" Payton held one up with a pair of tongs.

"You betcha."

His sister-in-law put four of them onto his plate and he found a seat on the stairs that led up to the twins' big combination bedroom and playroom.

Miles plopped down on the stair below him, baby Davy in his arms. East had mentioned that Miles was in the process of adopting Davy. Already father and son in the ways that mattered most, the baby and the big farmer looked good together. Miles caught Davy's fingers between his lips and the baby chortled in delight. "Da!" the kid crowed, well on his way to calling Miles Dad.

Through the stair rails he could see Alex. She'd snagged a coveted seat at the table. In a striped sweater and jeans, her gorgeous coffee-colored hair in loose waves down her back, she looked even better than his patty cake breakfast.

He answered her slow smile with one of his own.

"Uncle West!" Bailey called from the top of the stairs. "Come up. Play with us..."

"Give me a minute." He shoveled in the rest of his breakfast, took his plate to the sink and then went up to play video games with the boys.

Later, he and East drove into town to pick up a few things that somehow hadn't made anyone's Thanksgiving shopping lists. They needed whipping cream for the pies and mini marshmallows so there would be plenty for hot chocolate—and something called Kitchen Bouquet for the gravy.

When they got back from town, they joined the group at Marilyn's house. Marilyn's place was larger than the other two cottages. And a good thing, too. They totaled sixteen for dinner. By adding folding tables to both ends of Marilyn's oak table, they managed to seat everyone.

West and Alex were assigned to help the twins and Hazel create the Thanksgiving centerpiece.

Hazel knew her way around decorating a holiday table and Miles's fourteen-year-old came prepared. She brought baskets of what she called "fall floral" and a bunch of other decorations, too. There were orange candles, miniature pilgrim's hats, paper turkeys and small fake pumpkins. By the time they were finished, their masterpiece took up half the table.

Everybody gathered round to admire their work—and then Marilyn suggested gently that they would have to scale it down or there would be no room for the food. Bailey and Penn complained at first, but then they all got into the spirit of making it work on a less grandiose scale.

When they sat down to eat the table looked great. Ernesto said grace. As the amens went up around the table, West decided that all this family togetherness wasn't half bad. When he opened his eyes, the first thing he saw was Alex across from him, her dark head still bowed. When she looked up, he winked at her. She grinned in response and then scrunched up her nose, as if to say, *Isn't this great?—and stick to the rules, buddy. No flirting.*

He thought how much he liked her, followed immediately by how much he would love to have sex with her again. Yeah, he knew that wasn't going to happen.

But you can't blame a guy for dreaming.

West loaded up on turkey, stuffing and everything else. He had two slices of pie for dessert—one pumpkin, one pecan—and coffee spiked with Baileys Irish Cream. Around six, he and East and Ernesto went over to Payton's cottage to watch back-to-back football games. The others wandered in and out, watching for a while, then moving on. Payton came in with the boys at nine. They turned down the volume and she put the twins to bed.

It was after eleven when he finally returned to the guest cottage. Alex had left a lamp on in the living room. He turned it off and headed for bed.

In the little square of hallway, he noticed the faint light bleeding out from under Alex's door. For a good two minutes he stood in front of that door reminding himself that he wasn't going to knock. Then he knocked.

"It's open."

He pushed the door wide and found her propped up in bed, her hair in those yankable braids again. She had a thick book propped on her knees and big, black-framed sexy-librarian glasses perched on her nose.

"Good book?" he asked.

"It's a page-turner and a tearjerker, the kind of thing I never read."

"But is it good?"

"Oh, yeah. Can't put it down. Once I finish it,

I'm going to read all of Payton's books in order. I've heard they're really good, too. Josie and Auntie M have read them all. It's time I caught up." Payton wrote young adult fantasy. West had read one of them. It wasn't his thing, but he'd had no trouble finishing it—and he should say good-night and quietly shut the door.

"Come have a scotch with me."

She tipped her head to the side and scrunched her eyebrows together.

He put his hand to his ear. "Was that a yes?"

She set the book on the nightstand and laid her glasses on top of it. "Yes."

In the kitchen, she served them both a very nice single malt. "You want some crackers? Cheese?"

"After that amazing dinner and two slices of delicious pie? I'm good."

Just like last night, she took the stool next to him. He could get used to this.

She raised her glass. "To a good night's sleep."

He tapped his glass to hers and drank before confessing, "I drink scotch because I like it. Sleep's got nothing to do with it."

Her laugh had a snarky note to it. "To the truths that get told in the middle of the night."

So shoot him. Beyond the fact that he wanted to get naked with her again—he wouldn't, of course, but beyond what he wanted and wouldn't have, he did like her. She was fun and smart and straightforward. And it didn't hurt at all that she was so easy to look at.

He pointed at the index card on the fridge. "I love that you're living by fortune cookie wisdom."

She shoved the floppy sleeve of her sweater halfway up her arm. "Sometimes you just have to try something completely different."

"So then, you're getting a puppy or a kitten…"

"I have not committed to getting a pet."

"Duly noted, counselor. Ever been married?"

She scowled at him. "Who told you?"

He laughed. "It was a shot in the dark."

"You're kind of a brat, West."

"So I've been told—the ex. Talk."

Did he expect her to refuse? Yeah.

But she didn't. "I was twenty-three, in my first year of law school, when I met Devon Tate. He was also a law student. Devon was good-looking and charming, on law review. He had everything going for him. We dated for six months and then got married in Vegas. I think I knew it was a mistake as I was signing the marriage license. He was just like my dad, self-absorbed. It wasn't long before I found out he was also a cheater. I caught him at it a few months after we got married. I kicked him out and filed for divorce. That was the end of that."

"And you were done with men forever?"

"Please. Even with a dad who mostly pretended I didn't exist and Devon Tate for an ex-husband, I still had my dreams of finding The One."

"You're such a romantic."

She eyed him with skepticism and poured them each another two fingers of scotch.

He prompted, "So next you fell in love with…"

"His name was Rob Jensen. By then, I was living in Portland and I had been at Kauffman, Judd and Tisdale for two years. Rob worked as a barista at my favorite coffee place down the street from the office. A self-described homebody from Utah, Rob said he wanted only to be my support system. He was sweet, actually. I guess I was ready for someone who wanted to nurture me, you know?"

"I have to tell you, Alex. I'm stuck back there at 'a homebody from Utah.'"

"If you start laughing, I won't tell you the rest."

"Have I so much as cracked a smile?"

"You'd better not."

"Go on."

She gave him the side-eye, but at least she went on, "Rob and I agreed that I would make the money and he would make us a home. He cooked. He rubbed my back. We had bubble baths together, with candles! He told me how wonderful, strong and brilliant I was—but it didn't last."

"What happened?"

"He began to withdraw. Finally, he broke up with me because I was—his words—'stifling his soul' with my ambition and my drive."

"Tell me you kicked him out."

"I didn't have to. He left. He went back to Utah, got a job in his father's tractor sales business and married a nice hometown girl who couldn't wait to be a stay-at-home mom—which I know because he wrote me a letter telling me all about his wonderful, womanly bride, Lilith, who understood him and supported him and made him the kind of home he deserved—and what is that?"

He blinked. "What?"

"That look on your face."

"Alex, I don't know where to go with that story. What a wimpy-ass whiner dude."

"I look at it this way. Until the end, Rob was a very sweet guy. He never cheated, never ripped me off. He just thought he wanted to be a house husband and then he found out he was wrong. When he left, I was glad. It could have been a whole lot worse. But between Devon and Rob, I think I might be a little bit soured on relationships." She sipped her scotch. "Your turn."

He should have known she'd throw it back on him. "Wait. We're taking turns?"

"Evasions will get you nowhere with me. Your turn."

"What happened to the wonderful, understanding woman who came to my rescue last January?"

"You needed a wonderful, understanding woman last January. Right now, you just need to hold up your end of this conversation."

"So bossy," he muttered. "What's to tell? Someday, I want a family, kids. Not now, though. Now I like to keep things casual."

She set her drink on the countertop and turned the glass, slowly, in a circle. "So you want to be a family man, but right now you're a player?"

"No. Yes." He winced. "Maybe..." She laughed. He grumbled, "Oh, right. *You* can laugh, but I can't."

"Have you ever been married, West?"

He just might have winced again. "No."

She pointed at his face. "I saw that look. There's a story here. Tell me—wait."

"What?"

"Her name was Naomi, right?"

He shut his eyes and blew out a slow breath. "Payton told you."

When he looked at her again, she was nodding. "Remember that night Payton flew home from Seattle alone?"

"I do, yeah. All too well."

"That was the first night she met you and your parents. I picked her up at PDX and drove her here to the farm. On the way home, she told me about what had happened in Seattle, including the story about Naomi."

"Right. That was a bad night. Really bad. Poor Payton…"

"West."

He looked down into his drink and then back up at her. "The way you just said my name is not reassuring."

She only held his gaze, waiting.

He gave in. "I met Naomi Page seven years ago. We were dating casually for three or four months and then she tells me she's pregnant. She'd said she was on the pill and I always used a condom, so I didn't believe her. She swore I was the father and wanted a DNA test. We did the test. It showed that I was the father. I tried to step up. I tried to fall in love with her."

"You tried?" Alex's voice was gentle, soothing. Like that night last January.

He hated telling this story. "Okay, that sounds ridiculous."

"No. It doesn't. I think it's kind of sweet."

"Don't call me sweet." He felt like all kinds of fool.

She only said softly, "Please go on. Then what happened?"

"Well, I didn't fall in love with Naomi. But I really wanted that baby. I loved that baby and he wasn't even born yet. I started proposing—a lot. I proposed every chance I got. Naomi finally said yes—with some big financial stipulations. And as I'm guessing Payton already told you, the day of the wedding, the real father showed up. It was straight out of the movies, with the other guy standing up during the vows and swearing Naomi's baby was his. Naomi ordered the minister to get on with the ceremony, but that other guy seemed sincere to me. I refused to continue."

"You called off the wedding."

"Yeah. Until we could deal with the other man's claim. We did another test at a different lab. That test proved I wasn't the father, that Naomi must have somehow convinced someone at the first lab to fake the results. Turned out the guy who stood up at the wedding *was* the father. I ended up in a big legal wrangle with the lab that had handled the original test. They got slapped with some serious fines and people got fired. It was a complete mess."

Alex did that thing—leaning his way, bumping his arm with her shoulder. Like they were best buds. He really liked when she did that. She said, "You did everything you could, West. You put yourself out there. You did the right thing. It's not your fault that some woman tried to scam you."

"Yeah, but I bought her scam."

"It happens. From the way Payton told the story to me, your mom and dad bought Naomi's act, too."

"Yeah, it was heartbreaking for them when they found out they weren't grandparents, after all."

She nudged his arm again. "There's a silver lining in that story somewhere."

He realized she was right. "True, in a roundabout kind of way. Thanks to the baby's real father, Naomi didn't get away with her scam and I didn't end up married to a con artist. My folks were really let down. But eventually, they did get what they've always wanted. Two grandsons, a granddaughter on the way, Payton for a daughter-in-law and an excuse to spend most of their summers and just about every holiday right here on this farm that reminds them of those hazy, happy, long-ago days when they were growing up."

Alex didn't say a word. He knew she was only waiting for him to decide how much he wanted to reveal.

He went ahead and laid it out there. "It's a stretch, trying to pick out silver linings in the thing with Naomi. I was never that interested in finding that one special woman anyway. I had girlfriends, but never for all that long. I don't feel the connection the way my dad does with my mom, the way East does with Payton. And after the mess with Naomi, I've been even more careful to keep things strictly casual with women. I do want a family someday. I'm just not sure how that's going to happen because I don't really want to settle down." He couldn't read her expression—sad, maybe? Resigned? "Talk to me, Alex."

"I hear what you're saying. I get it. There needs to be so much trust to make a strong relationship. I can't see myself ever again trusting a man the way I trust Auntie M and my sisters."

"Wait a minute." He looked a little hurt. "Men are not all bad."

She chuckled. "Good to know."

"And, Alex, I do want to be married. I want to have children one of these days."

"Maybe you should try adoption, be a single dad..."

"Maybe. And I don't like it when you look at me like that."

"From what you've just told me, I don't believe you want to get married any more than I do."

"No, I *do* want to get married. Eventually..."

Again, she said nothing. She didn't have to. She called him a liar with her big brown eyes.

He muttered, "At least I'm willing to try. Maybe. Someday."

"What do you want me to say, West?"

That you believe me.

But he already knew she didn't. Props to her for keeping it honest.

Gathering the shreds of his manly dignity around him, he knocked back the last of his drink and stood. "Time for bed, I think."

She looked up at him and nodded. "Night, West. Sleep well."

Alex woke Black Friday morning to the doorbell ringing. She pulled on her cardigan and stuck her feet in her comfy Uggs. West poked his head out of his bedroom at the same time she did.

He gave her a sleepy smile. "Probably the twins," he guessed as one of the twins called out, "Aunt Alex, Uncle West! Wake up!"

They went to the door together.

The boys stood on the porch wearing pajamas, boots, matching puffy jackets and red hats with green pom-poms. Pink-cheeked and laughing, they were a matched pair of Christmas elves. And yet even though they were identical twins, she never had trouble telling them apart. It was the same with Easton and West. Each was so distinctly himself. Easton came across as more buttoned-up, a little bit preppy, his hair always perfectly trimmed at the nape. West wore his hair longer and had a sort of bad-boy vibe going on.

Bailey threw both arms wide. Behind him,

the ground was covered with a thin blanket of white. "We got snow!"

"Breakfast at our house!" Penn announced.

"C'mon and eat," instructed Bailey. "Then we can go get our Christmas trees!"

Laughing, they turned, ran down the steps and headed back to Payton's cottage, their boots leaving tracks in the new-fallen snow.

Alex shut the door.

West, in sweatpants and a thermal shirt, raked a hand back through his sleep-scrambled hair. "I'm surprised you're not out shopping already."

"I would have to drive to Portland to get the Black Friday retail experience. It's mostly farm co-ops and boutiques around here. There's plenty of fun shopping, but not before dawn."

"Wait a minute. Did Bailey say 'trees,' plural?"

"You must have missed the memo."

"No kidding." He crossed his arms over that broad chest of his. And she remembered that night last January. She'd raked her nails down his six-pack, feeling the hard ridges of muscle and… "Fill me in," he said.

Focus, she commanded her dirty mind. "Uh, we're decorating today. That includes all three cottages and a small tree in the motor home. Josie and her family will be decorating the big house at Halstead Farm. Your mom will whip the motor home into holiday shape in no time and then she'll help out wherever needed."

His gold eyebrows drew together. "My mom's helping out?"

"That's right. Something wrong with that?"

"She's just real particular about decorating for Christmas. Obsessively so—and are you saying that we're decorating the guest cottage, too?"

She laughed at his expression. "Get with the program, West. Yes. This cottage, too. That will be on you and me."

"Goody," he said with no enthusiasm whatsoever—but it was an act. His eyes had a certain gleam in them.

"You're into it. Don't lie—and don't worry, either. I'm sure we'll get help from the twins and from your mom."

"Yay," he said, faking grimness for all he was worth. "You have decorations for this?"

"Yep. Josie took most of hers over to the Halstead house, but she left a couple of boxes here. Your mom brought a bunch to share. Payton and Auntie M pitched in with some goodies for us, too. It's all up in the attic now."

"Ho, ho, ho," he grumbled.

"Still not fooled. You love it. You know you do."

West did love it. All the family togetherness crap really gave him the warm fuzzies in a big way. It brought back good memories of the Seattle house in Washington Park where he and East had grown up, the house his parents still lived in.

His mom had always been big on Christmas. She put up three trees. She baked cookies, made fudge and divinity, and wrapped an endless array of presents. Yeah, she needed everything to be perfect and that got on his last nerve sometimes, but she loved every minute of it and her enthusiasm was contagious.

Alex brushed his arm. "Better get moving. You can have the bathroom first. I'm assuming you'll make it quick."

An hour and a half later, they piled into four vehicles and caravanned to the Christmas tree lot. Miles Halstead, at the wheel of one of the farm trucks, led the way.

It took a while to choose six trees—two for the Halstead house, one each for the cottages and then a perfect three-foot noble fir for the motor home. They loaded all the trees onto the wide bed of Miles's truck and headed back to Wild Rose, where Miles circled the driveway, dropping off trees as he went.

After a short lunch break at the Halstead house, they got down to work.

In the guest cottage, West and Alex put the tree in the stand, brought down the boxes of decorations and hung the lights. Humming along with the Christmas tunes she streamed from the flat-screen over the fireplace, Alex made holiday magic with a grin on her face. He'd had more than one girlfriend who got really worked up over Christmas decorations, same as his mother. They wanted a guy's help, but they wanted everything just so.

Not Alex. She didn't even seem to notice that the lights weren't evenly distributed on every branch.

"There's a gap or two," he admitted reluctantly once all the lights were on—and then wondered what was wrong with him. He didn't care, so why even bring it up?

Alex shrugged. "Looks great to me."

He wanted to grab her and kiss her when she said that—hard, with tongue. And not only because she didn't care whether or not the lights were put on the tree just so. Honest truth? He wanted to kiss her—hard, with tongue—pretty much every time he glanced her way.

But he didn't. He wouldn't. Boundaries needed to be maintained. Somehow, they'd succeeded in positioning themselves solidly in the friend zone. Things could get weird if he stepped over the line.

"What?" She was frowning at him. "Weston, if you want to fiddle with the lights, go for it."

I want to fiddle with you. "On second thought, don't listen to me. Those lights look just right."

They'd started hanging the ornaments when his mother showed up.

West loved his mom and, yes, he had her to thank for all those bright, happy Thomas Kinkade–level Christmas memories. But his mom was the queen of Christmas decorating. And she ruled her Christmas kingdom with an iron hand—in a velvet glove, of course.

"Hey, Mom." West greeted her at the door.

She beamed him a big smile. "Help!" She had a wreath on one arm and a small, rolled-up rug under the other. In one hand she carried a door hanger—for the wreath, he assumed. "Look, sweetheart. It's snowing!" she announced and beamed a big smile. The snow had started falling again a little while ago. The wind was up, too. Her cheeks were pink.

"Gorgeous," he replied.

"Come out here," she instructed. "Shut the door."

He did as she ordered. Together, they rolled out a Christmas welcome mat and hung the wreath on the door. Inside, he helped her out of her heavy jacket and hung it up for her. She dropped her wool hat and gloves in the big basket by the door.

"We have a wreath and a Christmas welcome

mat," he said to Alex, and held up the everyday mat. "Where should I put this one?"

"Leave it right inside the door. It should fit there." He put the mat down. Alex hooked a crystal snowflake on the tree and asked, "Want some tea or hot chocolate, Joyce?"

"Thanks, but I had some tea before I walked over here." She sent a knowing glance from Alex to West and back to Alex again. "Now, how are you two doing together?"

Alex froze in the act of choosing the next ornament. She shifted her gaze to him, eyes wide and wary. Accusing, too. Like maybe she suspected he'd told his mother about what they'd been up to on East's wedding night.

He tried to look equal parts reassuring and innocent, though he felt vaguely insulted. He hadn't even told East. No way was his mother ever going to find out. "We're on the job here, Mom, no problem."

His mom put on her sweetest smile—the smile that said, *I'll be the judge of that*. "You're making great progress. But maybe a few minor readjustments to the lights, so they're evenly spaced, branch to branch..."

He slid a glance at Alex, who now seemed totally relaxed. Apparently, she'd realized his mom had no clue what the two of them had gotten up to the night East and Payton got married. Also,

Alex didn't seem to care in the least if Joyce Wright moved the lights around on the tree.

"Whatever you think, Joyce." She stepped aside so his mother could go to work.

For the next half hour, he and Alex hung ornaments on the sections of tree his mom had declared ready for decorations. The Christmas tunes played and the cottage smelled of cinnamon from the scented pine cones Alex had set on the coffee table in a red carnival glass bowl. His mom and Alex chatted about funny things Bailey and Penn had said and how fast baby Davy was growing.

"There." His mom stepped back to admire her work. "Perfect. I want to go check in with Marilyn and Ernesto next. You two all right to carry on without me?"

"I think we can manage, Mom."

She patted his cheek like he was the same age as his nephews, which annoyed him to no end—and then she laid her head on his shoulder with a little sigh. "Of course you can."

His heart kind of melted and he gave her a quick side hug. "The lights look great."

She beamed up at him. "They do, don't they?"

Two minutes later, she bustled out the door.

"I like your mom," said Alex, as they went back to work on the tree. "She puts it right out there, how she thinks things should be."

"Bugs the crap out of me sometimes."

"Yeah, I kind of picked up on that just now."

"She's so sweet, my mom—and so damn bossy." He slid a glance at Alex.

Her kissable mouth was twisted into a smirk. He had no doubt she was remembering that he'd called her bossy more than once. "You prefer meek, compliant women?"

"Oh, hell no. That's not what I said. You know I love my mom, but it's the way she's always so sweet about it while she's telling everyone what to do. That chaps my ass a little at times. If you're going to be bossy, just own it, you know?"

She pressed her lips together. He knew she was trying not to laugh. "Thank you for the clarification."

He considered a number of clever comebacks, but before he could decide which one to use, a pair of matching five-year-olds burst in the door.

"Aunt Alex, Uncle West, we're here!" shouted Bailey.

Shrugging out of his coat, Penn went up on his toes to hook it on a peg and crowed, "We'll help to do the decorating!"

"Inside voices, guys," Alex reminded them.

"Oops," Penn whisper-shouted, and hung his coat on top of his brother's.

"Sor-ry," said Bailey. "Do you have any candy canes?"

"Yes, I do," Alex replied, hanging the ornament in her hand and then turning for the kitchen.

"We *like* candy canes," Bailey added, just in case the adults hadn't gotten the message yet.

West stepped in then. "Help us get the rest of the decorations on the tree and we'll put on the candy canes last."

Penn peered up at him warily. "Why last?"

"And do we get to eat some?" No flies on Bailey. The kid got right to the point.

"Candy canes are the final touch," West explained.

"Who said that?" Penn wrinkled his nose.

"I did." Actually, his mom had always said that when he and East were little, followed by, "That way, you don't disturb any of the other ornaments when an adult gives you permission to eat one."

"Oh." Penn had that look. The conversation was not going as he'd hoped it might.

"But we do get to eat some, right?" Bailey tried again.

Alex returned from behind the kitchen island with a box of candy canes.

Penn sighed with happiness. "I want one, please, Aunt Alex."

Bailey seemed relieved. "Me, too, me, too!"

"I'll just check with your mom." Alex grabbed her phone and tapped out a quick text. A moment later, she had a reply. "Your mom says you may have one now and one after you've helped with the decorating."

The twins nodded in unison. "Okay!" they replied, also in unison.

Alex gave them each a candy cane.

Penn turned to West. "Would you help me to peel it so it doesn't get all broken?"

West helped Penn and then Bailey. Once they were both sucking their candy canes, they started grabbing for ornaments with already-sticky little fingers. He glanced at Alex, just to see if she would instruct them to eat their candy canes first and decorate afterward.

Alex shrugged. "What's Christmas without a few sticky ornaments?"

A half an hour later, she let them have their second candy canes. Attention spans pushed to the limit, they gobbled them up and announced that they'd better get going.

"Mom prob'ly needs us," Penn explained.

Alex reminded them to wash their hands, after which they put on their coats. West went out and stood on the porch. He watched them through the falling snow until they disappeared into the next cottage over.

Back inside, he pitched in to finish the tree. It was after five and already growing dark when they hung the last candy cane. They turned off all the lights except the ones on the tree and admired their work.

"It looks great," he said.

"Yeah. Really helped that your mom redistributed some of the lights, don't you think?"

"Right." He added drily, "I'm sure that made all the difference." Wrapping an arm around her—in a purely companionable way, of course—he gave her a squeeze. "You can't even tell which ornaments are sticky."

She looked up at him, grinning.

Damn. That mouth of hers seemed made for him. He wanted the taste of her, one more time.

Just one kiss.

What could it hurt?

He lowered his head. Her laughter ended on a quick, indrawn breath. She lifted her chin, which brought her lips closer—and his phone buzzed in his pocket.

"Oh!" She stepped back.

West dropped his arm from around her and pulled out the phone. "It's East. Dinner at six—at Josie's again."

She stared at him, her eyes so big and dark, her mouth softly parted. He imagined taking her plump lower lip between his teeth, biting it a little before sucking it into his mouth as he dragged her good and close against him.

"We should get going, then," she said in a small, worried voice.

"Right."

They put on their coats in silence and took separate cars.

Chapter Five

I can't believe I almost kissed him.

Through dinner at Josie's, Alex tried to keep her mind in the moment, to concentrate on the conversation, stay firmly in the now.

But she kept drifting away into some dreamy fantasyland where it was just her and West minus their clothes in a nice, big bed. She couldn't stop thinking about that moment when she'd looked up into his eyes—and the world just stopped. At that moment, she couldn't breathe. She'd almost reached for him.

If West's phone hadn't buzzed, she *would* have kissed him. And judging by that scorching hot look in his eyes, he would have kissed her back. After that, well, she had a very strong feeling they wouldn't have stopped with just that one kiss.

Because no matter how hard she tried to remember that it would be foolish in the extreme to end up in his arms again, she hadn't forgotten how great it was with him. Weston Wright, by his own admission, might be a bad bet as a boyfriend. But the man knew how to treat a woman when he had her in his bed.

Not that it mattered.

It didn't. Uh-uh. Not to her. It wasn't going to happen again. She needed not even to let herself consider that it might happen again. Where could it go but somewhere difficult and awkward? She didn't want a relationship and neither did he.

And that could be good, right? whispered a naughty voice inside her head. They could enjoy each other for Thanksgiving and Christmas and then just walk away.

But wait. It would be far too easy to slip up. Someone in the family would probably find out…

Well, so what? Maybe they would all just mind their own business.

Yeah, and Santa really did come down the chimney every Christmas Eve.

Their one-night stand had hurt no one. He'd needed it and she'd loved it—not only the great sex, but also the honesty, the connection. She'd loved *all* of it. And the next morning they'd both used good sense and walked away.

Getting into it with each other again? That would be tempting fate, pure and simple.

After dinner, Ernesto suggested a poker game over at Auntie M's. The men and Auntie M took him up on it. Everyone else hung out at Josie's until midnight. They streamed a couple of Disney movies, ate popcorn and drank hot cider. When the twins conked out, the women, including Ashley and Hazel, watched a Hallmark Christmas movie. Around midnight, the party broke up.

Alex drove back to Wild Rose. When she parked her Audi beside the cottage, West's rental car was already there in the space next to hers. The tree looked gorgeous and welcoming in the front window.

She paused at the foot of the steps. With the snow coming down, a wreath on the door and that tree in the window, the little house was the perfect Christmas cottage. It looked nothing short of magical.

Inside, though, the rooms were dark. West's bedroom door stood open. Nobody home.

Alex took a quick shower and went to bed. Around two, she heard him come in. She almost tossed back the covers and ran out into the main room to…

What, exactly?

Ask him if he would like some Sleepyhead Tea?

Or grab him and kiss him and drag him back to her room?

Nope. No way. Not going to happen.

She had to stop thinking about it and try her best to avoid him. Yeah, fine. They were roomies in a small cottage, sharing a bathroom the size of a postage stamp, mutually prone to getting up in the middle of the night and hanging around in the kitchen together.

But staying away from him could be done. And by God, she would do it.

He helped by being gone when she got up at nine Saturday morning. She ate a light breakfast alone. That afternoon, she and her sisters took the kids to Heartwood Holiday Market right there in town at Heartwood Brewery. Local farmers and crafters filled the top floor of the big, modern brewery and sold Christmas crafts and holiday treats.

That night, Easton, West and their dad drove into town for burgers and beers. Payton had Alex and Josie over for dinner, a sisters' night in. Miles was looking after Davy. Joyce had the twins in the motor home for a sleepover.

Josie talked about having more kids. "At least

two. We'll adopt one and maybe try for one more pregnancy."

Payton groaned and rubbed her big belly. "Adoption. Why didn't we think of that?"

Josie chuckled. "Because making them is fun?"

Payton turned to Alex. "What about you, big sister? You used to talk about having kids."

"Not for several years, I haven't." She took a slow sip of the delicious red wine Payton had served with dinner. "Not since I divorced Devon, anyway..."

"Devon Tate." Payton snort-laughed. "There's a blast from the past."

"What a dog," muttered Josie. Alex and Payton nodded in agreement.

Devon had not only cheated, but he'd also made passes at both Josie and Payton during the one time Alex had brought him home to the farm. Her sisters had spoken to her separately. They were both miserable to have to tell her such a thing about the man she'd married.

When Alex confronted him for putting moves on her sisters, he'd called them a couple of lying bitches and stormed out. She'd known then that it was over and started sleeping on the couch. A couple of weeks later, she came home early and caught him in their bed with someone else.

That did it. She'd moved out of their apartment and filed for divorce.

"As for kids," said Alex, "I don't know. I really don't. I admit I'm thinking it about it, though—especially in the past week, after I walked out of KJ&T."

"You'd be a great mom," said Payton.

Josie nodded. "Yes, you would."

Payton said, "And I keep meaning to ask how it's working out, being roomies with Weston?"

Alex was ready for that one. "It's good. He's easygoing, helpful. Picks up after himself. He's great with children…"

Were her sisters looking at her strangely?

Nah. She was just being paranoid. Nobody knew that she couldn't stop thinking of jumping her sister's husband's brother—again.

Like the night before, he wasn't there when she got back to the guest cottage. And that was good—wonderful. She washed her face, brushed her teeth and was all tucked in bed with Payton's first book when she heard him come in. She stayed tucked in bed.

All through that night.

In the morning, she woke to the smell of coffee.

West tapped on her door. When she stuck her head out, he asked, "Want some eggs? I'm cooking."

Oh, what the hell? "Scrambled. Wheat toast."

"Done."

She pulled on some clothes, turned on the tree lights and set the table. They ended up drinking way too many cups of coffee as they brainstormed her options for a new career.

It was so much fun, sitting across from him, debating the merits of journalism versus becoming a mediator—in the court system *or* the private sector. She could try marketing or consulting.

"The possibilities are endless," he said. "You could become a CFO, just like me."

"I'll drink to that." She got up and poured them each more coffee.

By eleven o'clock, when Payton texted her to come out to the event barn and help with the final preparations for Kyle and Olga's wedding that night, Alex had concluded that she really had no reason to keep avoiding West. They'd been sharing the cottage since Wednesday and he'd yet to make a single move—because that almost-kiss Friday night? It hadn't happened, so it didn't count.

Nothing was going to happen. They both knew better than to start that kind of trouble. And he would be out of here tomorrow, on his way back to Seattle.

"Payton wants my help with the wedding tonight," she said as she stuck her phone back in her pocket.

"Go ahead," said West. "I'll clean up the kitchen."

Not only was the man way too hot and fun to hang with, but he also cooked and cleaned up after himself, too. If he ever got over his aversion to lasting relationships, some woman someday was going to get really lucky.

"Thank you," she said. "For breakfast, for the career brainstorming *and* for doing the dishes."

"No problem. I needed to remind you what a great roomie I am. Christmas is coming. I can't have you suddenly deciding you need this cottage all to yourself. I could end up in the motor home with my parents. I can't do that again. After last time, I'm already scarred for life."

"No worries," she promised. "You'll always have the back bedroom here."

The bride, Olga Balanchuk, had hired a wedding planner. That made everything easier. The wedding planner had staff who would set up and serve.

But Kyle Huckston, the groom, was a close family friend. If help was needed on Wild Rose or Halstead Farm, the Huckstons were the first to show up and get to work. In appreciation for all the years of friendship and support, Payton and

Josie wanted to add a few extra touches to Kyle and Olga's wedding.

They'd rented beaded crystal chandeliers—a dozen of them, to hang from the rafters and light up the wintry night. They'd draped yards and yards of glimmer illusion tulle overhead, too. Twinkle lights were everywhere, spilling down the walls, woven in and out of all that glittery tulle.

Alex worked alongside her sisters and the wedding planner's crew until three thirty, when she returned to the guest cottage to get ready for the wedding ceremony at five.

West wasn't there, which was great. She had the small house all to herself. She could run back and forth from the bathroom to the bedroom in her underwear without giving West the wrong signal.

When she returned to the barn, most of the guests had already arrived and taken their seats. She found an empty chair in the second-to-last row between Delia Morton, who owned a restaurant in town, and Rafe Jenks, who had been working with Miles at Halstead Farm for as long as Alex could remember. She and Rafe exchanged greetings and then Delia started talking—about how gorgeous the barn looked, so romantic and magical.

"And isn't the music just splendid?" Delia

rattled right on without waiting for an answer. "That's Payton's doing, right?" Payton was endlessly creative. Not only did she write bestselling stories, she played guitar and knew all the local musicians. She'd gone to high school with the wedding's pianist and she used to sit in with the band that would play during the reception. "And I have to say, your sister looks like she might pop that baby out any minute now, doesn't she?"

"Delia, she's not due until mid-January."

"Well, you coulda fooled me. And she does have that glow. So romantic, the way she and her husband found each other after all those years apart…"

There was more. About Josie and Miles. "The perfect match, those two. I'm surprised they didn't get together long ago—and yes, I realize he was married before and he is a bit older than Josie. So I have to admit, there's really no way they could have gotten together much sooner than they did. I'm just so glad they've found each other at last."

Next, she quizzed Alex about her life in Portland—as always, never pausing long enough to get an answer to any of her questions. "You are such a go-getter, Alexandra. Really just nothing short of admirable. But what about love, honey? Someone special in your life? It's a challenge, I'm sure, balancing a demanding career and a meaningful relationship, but it can be done and I do believe it's very much worth the effort..."

At least she shut up when the pianist switched from light prelude music to Pachelbel's Canon in D. Even Delia Morton fell reverently silent for that.

It was beautiful, that ceremony. Mostly because Kyle was the happiest man alive and Olga looked like a Norse princess in her cream-colored boho wedding dress, carrying a glorious bridal bouquet of pampas grass, eucalyptus leaves and roses in the colors of fall—burnt orange, mustard yellow and terra-cotta red.

By the time the groom kissed the bride, there was hardly a dry eye in the barn. Alex didn't often get emotional at weddings, but the sheer happiness radiating from both Olga and Kyle just might have made her mascara run—a little.

Next came the meal, a buffet set up on the other side of the barn. The wedding planner's crew got to work clearing the chairs on the ceremony side for the dancing later. A server circulated with flutes of sparkling wine—the good stuff, Mumm Napa. Alex took one and savored her first sip.

Several feet away, on the far side of the buffet table, West stood chatting with a pretty blonde woman Alex didn't recognize. The woman laughed, throwing her head back, as if West had just said something hysterically funny. Alex took another sip of bubbly—a bigger one this time.

As she lowered the half-empty flute, West just happened to glance her way. He gave her that wry smile of his and raised his flute to her. She saluted him back. The unknown woman reached out and brushed his sleeve to regain his attention. Alex looked away and sipped more sparkling deliciousness.

Really, she needed to pace herself with the bubbly wine. The night was young.

She mingled, catching up with old school friends, most of whom were married now, some with kids in their early teens. In a way, it made her feel a little sad. She'd walked out on her big-time career and Delia Morton was right. She'd never found what Josie had with Miles, what Payton and Easton shared.

But hey. She wasn't dead yet. Love could still find her. Consider Auntie M, widowed for years and years. And then, finally, she'd allowed herself to take a chance on Ernesto.

Alex looked down. Her champagne glass was empty. She set it on the tray of a passing server and went to get something to eat before grabbing another.

And as for finding love, maybe she did need to be more open to the possibility that there actually might be someone out there for her. Maybe she needed to stop telling herself that men were nothing but trouble—oh, and get a puppy.

Yes. A full-time commitment to another living being. That would be a nice start. Finding a man could wait until she'd at least figured out what to do with the rest of her life.

She ate with Josie and Miles, baby Davy and their girls. Ashley had brought her boyfriend, Chase, who was almost as handsome as Ashley was beautiful. Chase clearly had it bad for Ashley. The two of them were adorable together, holding hands under the table, sharing tender glances, but still putting in the effort to make nice with the family.

After dinner, Alex allowed herself another flute of bubbly. She had cake and coffee. And another sparkling wine when the dancing started—kicked off by the bride and groom letting it all hang out to Ed Sheeran's "Put It All on Me."

By nine or so, parents had corralled their kids and whisked them off to bed. Alex danced with Myron Wright and the groom. She was standing on the sidelines enjoying the music when someone spoke from behind her.

"Alex?" She turned. Aaron Black, whom she'd dated briefly in high school, held out his hand. "You look ah-mazing. Dance with me?" She hesitated. She and Aaron had not parted on good terms. "Aw, c'mon, Alex. It's been years..."

Against her better judgment, she let him lead her out on the floor. She should have at least waited for a fast song. As they danced, she learned he was on his second divorce and as handsy and brash as ever. His fingers strayed below her waist. She pulled back twice and reminded him that he'd better behave, or else.

"Sorry. You're just irresistible."

"And you are pushing it. Stop."

For the next couple of minutes, he kept his hands where they belonged. The dance was almost finished. She couldn't wait to get away from him. The song finally faded off.

And there was West, tapping on Aaron's shoulder. Aaron had a look like he might actually attempt to hold her captive for the next dance.

Alex shrugged free of his grip and reached gratefully for West. "There you are." She blasted him a giant smile as the next song began. He danced her away from Aaron.

"Who was that tool?" he asked in her ear.

Had he been watching her? She breathed in the scent of him and decided that she liked the idea of him looking out for her. She liked it so much!

"His name's Aaron Black," she said. "I went to high school with him. We went on two dates.

The first was okay. The second date, not so much. The guy was an octopus with the hands. I lectured him on the meaning of the word *no* and refused to go out with him again."

"Apparently, he's a slow learner."

"Sadly, you may be right." She really wanted to ask about the pretty woman at the buffet table. But she knew she shouldn't—and then she did it anyway. "For a minute there, I thought you'd met someone."

He frowned down at her. "Met someone, how?"

Too late to back out now. "The pretty blonde woman you were talking to before dinner."

"Oh, yeah." He smirked. "Jealous?"

"West," she chided, "that's not who we are."

"Right." He seemed to be trying not to grin. "She seemed like a nice woman."

"Just nice? She looked really interested to me."

"You *are* jealous."

She scoffed. Loudly. "Dream on."

When the dance ended, he took hold of her hand. She laced her fingers with his. They got more wine, hung out with Auntie M and Ernesto for a while, danced some more.

Now, with West beside her, the night seemed full of promise. The twinkle lights and chandeliers overhead shone brighter than before. At midnight, the bride threw her fabulous bouquet.

The pretty blonde who'd flirted with West at the beginning of the evening caught it. Kyle and Olga rode off in a carriage drawn by two white horses.

Inside the barn, the party continued. The sparkling wine flowed freely. Alex enjoyed it all—the party *and* the wine. West seemed to be having a pretty good time, too.

By one, Alex's sisters and their husbands had left the party. Auntie M and Ernesto, too. Myron and Joyce had headed back to their motor home.

Alex excused herself to use the new, larger ladies' room on the back side of the event barn. She'd had the restrooms expanded and upgraded last summer, along with putting in an HVAC system, paving the dirt driveway from the barn to the main road and adding a coatroom in front.

As she washed her hands, reapplied lip gloss and finger-combed her hair, she grinned at herself in the pretty gold-framed mirror. She was having the best night ever.

And she'd just had a fabulous idea.

"Champagne courage." She clucked her tongue at herself in the mirror, keeping her voice low even though nobody else was in the restroom right then. "You really shouldn't. You need to behave..."

But then she found West waiting right there outside the door when she left the ladies' room.

He looked exactly like her favorite forbidden secret fantasy.

She took his hand. "Come with me."

"Where?"

She moved in close and pressed herself shamelessly right up against him. He felt so good—hard and broad and all man. Leaning up, she whispered in his ear, "Time to go."

"But where?"

"Back to the guest cottage—and don't look so puzzled. It's a wedding."

"Well, yeah…"

"Are you saying you don't remember what we do after a wedding?"

Those blue eyes got even bluer and that mouth of his curled up at one corner. "Alex. Are you sure?"

"Do I look uncertain?" Still on tiptoe, she breathed the words against his lips. "Because I'm not."

A low huff of breath escaped him—like a bull about to charge. The sound sent shivers ricocheting all through her. His mouth met hers.

Oh, that kiss. It started out cautious, carefully restrained, as though he wanted to kiss her hard and deep, but he just wasn't sure.

She made it her mission to wipe every doubt from his mind. When his tongue tempted hers, she didn't hesitate. She twined her arms around his neck and pulled him closer, sliding her tongue past his parted lips, drinking in that groan of his that told her everything she needed to know. His arms banded tighter as she melted against him.

When he lifted his head, his eyes had gone feral. "Let's go, then." Three simple words. But the way he said them—all rough and hungry, impatient and maybe a little bit angry. Like he hadn't meant to do this.

But he just couldn't stop himself.

She got that. She did. She felt the same way.

He grabbed her hand and pulled her toward the barn doors.

Chapter Six

He'd tried to resist her, tried his best to take the high road for five whole days and four endless nights.

Tonight, though. Impossible.

So to hell with the high road. He wanted her. She wanted him. It was only one more night. He needed it—another night, a second night minus all the pain and the sadness. A purely happy night to add to that other night he would never forget.

Really, what could it hurt? He was leaving early in the morning. By Christmas—when the family would no doubt insist they share the cottage once again—tonight would be only a memory. One both of them would do their best to forget.

Yeah. It would all be just fine.

They had to stop at the barn door to give the coat-check guy their tickets. He came back with their heavy coats—and shiny black knee-high rubber boots for her, the kind made to fit over her sexy high-heeled shoes. He thought of that night at the first of the year, of the two of them at the side of the road. She'd had no rubber boots that night. For his sake, she'd gotten mud on her pretty satin shoes.

They left the barn and set out along the dirt road to the circle of small houses, each with a tree shining bright in the front window. The sky overhead, thick with stars, was clear of clouds for once, the same midnight blue as her dress. A crescent of moon glowed down at them.

The road was lumpy, dotted with frozen clumps of mud and dirty snow. They wrapped their arms around each other and forged ahead, laughing.

At the cottage, they waited until they got inside to fall all over each other. He slammed the door behind him and grabbed her. She grabbed right back and shoved her mouth up to his.

He took those beautiful, plump lips of hers, kissing her like a starving man as he ripped off his own coat, dropped it on the floor and shoved hers off right after it.

They left a trail of rubber boots, shoes, socks and coats behind them as they headed for the small square of hallway. Kissing madly, stopping mid-step to pull off some random article of clothing, they grabbed each other tight again, crashing together in another long, hot kiss before taking yet another step.

In the hallway, she fisted the lapels of his suit jacket. Moaning as she kissed him, she yanked him backward through the open door of her room. Halting on the rug beside the bed, she pulled back and demanded, “Condoms?”

“Wallet,” he growled. Unfortunately, his wallet was in the inside pocket of his winter coat, which they'd left back there by the front door. “And there's a boxful in my room…”

She kissed him again, hard and quick. “You knew this would happen,” she accused. “You came prepared.”

Well, not consciously. Should he confess—or deny it?

Before he could choose which way to go, she gave him a push. “Get the box.”

He did, returning in seconds flat. She hadn't wasted a moment. He found her sitting on the edge of the turned-back bed. The curve-hugging blue dress was gone. Now she wore only a black thong and a lacy black strapless bra.

He took three condoms from the box and laid them close at hand as she hooked slender fingers under the waistband of his trousers and opened her legs enough to pull him between them.

She tipped her face up to him, her soft mouth curving in a welcoming smile, those velvet brown eyes so deep, full of promise, ready for anything. "Where were we?"

As if she had to ask. His belt, tie and shirt were already strewn back there on the floor somewhere. She had his pants down in a flash. And then he couldn't wait. He guided his boxer briefs over his straining erection and shoved them down and off, as well.

Crooking a finger at him, she scooted backward.

He joined her on the bed. She laughed and then she gasped as he caught hold of her. They wrestled briefly; her long, thick hair, pinned up on one side in a tangle of dark curls, got loose and spilled all around them. He needed to wrap a big hank of that hair around his hand, pull her head back, take that mouth again…

In a minute. First, he managed to reach around behind her and unhook her bra.

She shoved at him playfully. "Augh, you're too quick."

"Don't worry. I can be slow when it counts." He planted a hard kiss on those fine lips and threw the lacy bra over his shoulder.

At last, he had both of those beautiful breasts of hers in his hands, where they fit just right.

And in his mouth.

She moaned in welcome as he palmed one and bit the nipple of the other. How had he lasted this long without grabbing her and manhandling her again?

The way she felt, just as he remembered, all silky and strong, pulling him so close, kissing him like she would never get enough.

He couldn't get enough of her, either—after tonight, it would be even harder than before to keep from kissing her, holding her, making her his again.

So what? He was here with her now, free to touch her, to hold her, to lick all her secret places. He planned to make her beg, make her shout his name when it mattered most—which was pretty much constantly, for the rest of the night.

She surprised him, getting one foot planted firmly on the bed somehow, giving a good, hard push—and ending up on top. "Ha! Who's the boss now?" She got right down in his face, her hair tumbling everywhere, sliding against his cheek, pooling on his shoulder.

He stared in those eyes he occasionally—really,

not *that* often—saw in his dreams, deepest brown ringed in amber. "You're the boss, Alex," he answered, deadpan. "Be nice."

That made her laugh—and gave him the advantage. He rolled until he topped her again. And then he kissed her. He took his time about it, sliding a hand down her hair, getting hold of a nice big handful, wrapping it slowly around his fist. Her scent was everywhere, musky and rich.

She whispered, "West," against his lips, not pleading exactly—not yet.

He had her hair coiled around his hand now, so he used it, tugging her head back with it, letting his mouth wander over the obstinate jut of her chin, down the silky slope of her throat to the delicate curves of her collarbones.

And lower—though not by much. He couldn't resist detouring for a bit when he reached those glorious breasts again—two handfuls, just right. He palmed them, sucking one and then the other into his eager mouth as she urged him on with soft pants and hungry cries, clutching his shoulders, walking her fingers down the muscles of his back until she could grab his ass and hold on tight.

She whispered, "Yes!" and then she used the word to beg him a little. "Yes, West. Yes, please… Now, West. Oh, please…"

He got moving again, down over her pretty

belly and the gentle slope of her mound, so neatly trimmed, a cute strip of dark hair pointing the way to his destination. Taking her sleek thighs in either hand, he lifted them and spread them wide so that he could get his shoulders between them.

She was already so wet, totally ready. But he wasn't rushing this. He only had this one more night with her. Everything he did with her needed to be savored, thoroughly enjoyed.

So he savored. In depth. At length.

She speared her fingers into his hair, pulling it, pleading with him. "West, come on. I can't wait any longer. West, I do need you. I need you now. Please. I need you now..."

He really did like it when she begged. It had happened so rarely in his limited experience of her—right now and on that dark night last January. A man had to seize his moment. Carpe diem, for sure. He took his time with her until she came, pulsing so sweetly against his tongue. He kissed her slow and gentle, nipping a little and then using the flat of his tongue, until she went limp with a long, happy sigh.

And then, well, she tasted so good. And she looked like heaven, spread out on the bed for him. He couldn't resist making her come again. The second time was quicker, yet equally sweet.

What was it about her that revved him up so high? Strength, maybe? Power. She was a force to be reckoned with. But she was kind at the core. And loyal. There was nothing she wouldn't do for her sisters, her aunt, her nieces and nephews—for his family, too, now. For all the people *her* people loved.

A queen. That was Alex. Benign and generous—until she had to be otherwise to protect what mattered to her.

"West." Her voice was soft now. Her fingers stroked, slow and sweet, through his hair. "West, that was…so good. So, so good."

He looked up into those eyes of hers, the pupils blown wide with pleasure. Her cheeks and upper chest were flushed a sweet rosy hue. Her hair, in dark tangles, spread out on the pillow.

"So good," she whispered, her eyes droopy. Sated. "Did I mention that already?"

He scooted up a little and pressed a kiss to the tender flesh of her belly as a soft chuckle escaped her.

"Not done," he informed her. Resting his head between her hip bones, he traced a slow spiral on the silky skin of her upper thigh. "This will take until daylight, at least."

She sighed. "What time are you leaving for Seattle?"

"I'm out the door at seven." After they dropped the rental cars off in Hood River, he was riding home in Payton's giant nine-seater SUV with

Payton, the kids and East. The parents would follow in the motor home. Family togetherness. Nothing quite like it—but that was hours away. "We've got plenty of time."

He heard her sigh. She traced the tip of her finger down the bridge of his nose. When she touched his lips, he nipped at her. She giggled like a kid, delighted and free.

And suddenly, he was aching for her, wanting her, needing her.

Rising up, he grabbed for a condom, got rid of the wrapper and rolled it down over his ready length.

She reached for him. He went into her outstretched arms, his breath catching as she pulled him close, one arm easing between them, finding him, guiding him right to where he wanted to be.

"Alex." A push of his hips and he was there—surrounded by heat and wetness, her body tight and yet giving way, letting him in. "Alex…"

She made soft sounds, hungry, eager sounds. He buried his face in the fragrant curve of her neck. She wrapped her legs around him, pulling him tighter, closer, until he filled her completely.

Holding him, surrounding him, she gave herself up to him. He pulled back enough to watch her eyes as he wrapped his arms around her and rolled them, ending up on the bottom, giving her the control.

"Yes," she whispered, her hair falling forward as she sat up and folded her legs under her. Tucking her calves close to his sides, skin to skin, she rode him. Her body rocked him as she moved on him. She tossed her head back, all that glorious hair falling in dark coils over the flushed skin of her breasts, along the smooth, strong lengths of her arms.

"I'm close," he warned.

"Wait. Please…" she begged so sweetly.

"Can't. Uh-uh. No way…"

She bent close and kissed him, her lips soft. Hot. Inviting.

He took her face between his hands and kissed her right back, spearing his tongue in to meet hers. They groaned together, the sound an echo of pure pleasure inside his head.

"Oh, West." Her breath on his face, her lips brushing his as she instructed, "Like this. Just like this…"

Holding on by a thread, he caught her lower lip between his teeth and bit down—not too hard, just enough to bring another desperate, needful cry from her, to push her right to the edge. "Now, Alex," he commanded. "Come, sweetheart. Come now…"

And she did. With a low cry, she threw her head back and let go. Somehow he held out until she hit the crest. After that, it was all over. He lost it completely. Surging up into her, he let go, too.

Sometime later, she flopped down on top of him with a long, happy sigh. He wrapped his arms around her. There was peace, for a little while.

Then, carefully, he rolled and took the top position. With care, he withdrew and got up to dispose of the condom.

When he returned, she was sitting on the edge of the bed, still naked, grinning. "I was just thinking about ice cream," she said.

He put on sweats and she grabbed a robe from the back of her bedroom door. They went out to the kitchen, sat at the island and shared a pint of Ben & Jerry's chocolate chip cookie dough.

Revived, they returned to the bedroom and reached for each other. He needed to make love to her again. And again. They only had this one more night and he refused to waste a single moment.

Sometime before dawn, she fell back against the pillows with a groan. "I'm just going to shut my eyes for a minute..."

He pulled her close and kissed the top of her head. "I wore you out."

She punched him lightly on the arm. "Braggart." And then she yawned. Her eyes fluttered shut.

And her breath evened out.

He turned off the light and shut his eyes, too, but not for long. At six, careful not to disturb her,

he left the bed. For a few minutes, he crept around, trying to be quiet while he gathered up his clothes from the rug and in the tiny square of hallway and out in the main room. Before he cleaned up and got dressed, he pulled her door shut to keep from waking her.

By 6:55 he was showered, packed and ready to go. He took his big suitcase and laptop out to the main room, leaving them by the front door. Now he debated—leave a note to let her know how amazing she was? Or wake her up and say goodbye?

He hated to wake her, but the note seemed—what? Not enough?

Yeah. That.

He tapped on her door.

"It's open."

He pushed it inward to find her sitting against the headboard, the covers drawn up over those fine round breasts. She looked rosy and sleepy, her hair every which way. His dick twitched in his pants.

She asked softly, "On your way out?"

Damn. He was out of control when it came to her, aching to rip off his clothes and jump right back in that bed with her all over again. Why? He'd spent hours last night crawling all over her. He should be more than ready to be on the move. "Yeah. I need to get over to Payton's."

She nodded. “Have a safe ride home, West.”

“Thanks.” He gulped. “Alex, I…”

“Say it.” She gazed at him through lazy, satisfied eyes.

“I left the key in the utility drawer.”

“Okay…”

“Also…”

“I’m listening.”

“I loved it,” he said flatly.

One of her eyebrows hitched up and she looked at him sideways. “You don’t sound like you loved it.”

“It’s only…”

“What?” Now she was the one speaking with zero inflection.

“Well, we shouldn’t have. We broke our own rule. I feel pretty bad about that.” Did he? Really?

Not in the least.

But he did feel strangely desperate.

The truth came at him like a runaway train. *I don’t want to go.*

What in the ever-loving hell was happening here?

He’d never been the guy who didn’t want to go. “We just have to be…smarter, that’s all.”

She wore a thoughtful expression—and even that turned him on. “Smarter,” she repeated, frowning a little.

Why did she have to look at him like that? She

was driving him crazy, sitting there in the tangled bed, naked under the covers, her hair all over the place, looking all kinds of hot and cuddly and… right.

"West." The frown vanished. It morphed into a slow, drowsy smile.

He folded his arms across his chest to keep from reaching for her, to stop himself from jumping back into that bed with her.

Lazily, she yawned and slowly brought up her hand to cover her mouth. He just stared. She was yanking his chain, he knew that. He resented her for doing that.

At the same time, well, she could yank his chain all she wanted. As long as she let him…

What?

Hold her again, kiss her some more…

Spend half the day, at least, tucked up nice and cozy, together with her in bed…

She chuckled. "What's on your mind, West? You can tell me."

"Well, I should get going, get over to Payton's."

She put a on a pouty face, really hamming it up. "And here I was hoping for a Christmas affair…"

He blinked and all the air fled his lungs. Was she serious?

She's messing with you, fool, he reminded himself yet again. *You're acting like a spoiled frat boy and Alex Herrera has no patience for jerks.*

She might be playing it seductive and teasing, but underneath the teasing he saw…

What?

Annoyance? Anger? Exasperation?

He wasn't quite sure what to call that look on her face. But she was not happy with him and he couldn't stand that. His mind spun like a hamster on a wheel as he tried to figure out how to salvage this situation.

The doorbell rang.

And he copped out. "Uh, that'll be Easton. I have to go."

She stared at him way too steadily now. "Have a safe trip home, West." Icicles dripped from every word.

"Thanks." Spinning on his heel, he made for the front door.

Alex didn't move a muscle. She heard the murmur of male voices from the other room, followed by suitcase wheels bumping over the threshold and the sound of the front door clicking shut. For a minute or two more, she hesitated, sitting absolutely still until West's car started up outside.

Only then did she burst into action, shoving back the covers, leaping from the bed. Grabbing her robe off the back of the door, she pulled it on and wrapped it around her as she scooted to the window.

Between the shut blinds, she watched West's rental car pull to a stop in front of Payton's cottage. Easton jumped out and climbed in the other rental car. With Payton's big SUV leading the way, Easton falling in behind her, West behind him and the Wright parents' motor home taking up the rear, the caravan of vehicles set out.

Once the motor home disappeared from sight, Alex sank back to the bed and buried her face in her hands. "Dear God in heaven. I can't believe I said that. A Christmas affair?" A whimper escaped her. "What is the matter with me?"

Nothing is the matter with you, she sternly reminded herself as she yanked at the belt on the robe to tie it nice and tight.

It had been a great night. The *best* night. And this morning, West had flat-out pissed her off. She didn't need his apologies. He could stuff his regrets right up that fine ass of his.

And when he showed up for Christmas, he could damn well sleep in the motor home with his oversexed parents or get a room at the Heartwood Inn.

She fell back across the bed with a sigh.

Okay, just possibly she was being too hard on him.

Last night had been intense, to say the least. Maybe he'd freaked out a little bit—same as she had just now.

She would try not to hold it against him. So much of the time she'd spent with him the past few days had been great. He'd helped her, he really had. Their talks had her feeling so much better about herself and her future. She owed him for that.

Plus, well, the look on his face when she'd offered to be his lover just for the holidays?

Priceless.

She sat up, laughed and flopped back across the wrinkled sheets again.

Okay, fine. He'd pissed her off, but she still liked him. A lot.

And maybe a few weeks from now, when he showed up for Christmas, she wouldn't say no to him taking the back bedroom for the holiday.

And here I was hoping for a Christmas affair...

All through the long ride home, as his nephews bickered, demanding potty breaks and/or french fries every half hour, West stared blindly out his side window and thought about Alex and that offer she'd made him.

Did she mean it even a little?

Or was she only mocking him for making an ass of himself over last night?

Alex...

He grinned out the window as they crossed the Columbia River into Washington State. He'd had a really good time with her.

And not just last night, either.

He liked how strong and capable and honest she was. He couldn't get enough of the way she put it right out there. She was a powerful woman.

And yeah, he was more than a little intimidated by everything about her—but not intimidated enough to stop imagining the great time they could be having if he'd only had the presence of mind to jump right on her offer of a holiday fling.

"Hold that thought," he should have said, and then informed East that he wouldn't be driving home with the family, after all.

True, she might have laughed in his face if he'd taken her seriously. So what? He should have gone with it anyway, just on the off chance she'd meant what she said.

A french fry hit him on the cheek—thrown by Penn, who cackled in delight at his own bad behavior and then instantly became contrite, complete with sad, puppy-dog eyes. "Oops. Sorry, Uncle Weston."

"Settle down, back there," commanded East from the front seat.

West ate the french fry. "No harm done."

* * *

Alex put on her reindeer pajamas and went back to bed. Why not?

Thanksgiving had been action-packed on so many levels. A day or two lazing around wouldn't hurt. She got up at eleven, ate a sandwich and thought about West's suggestion that she adopt a pet. Vaguely, she recalled that Heartwood Animal Rescue had regular pet adoption drives. Would there be one over the holidays?

She looked online and marked the date—this coming Saturday. She might not be having a hot holiday affair with her sister's husband's brother—but at least she could find a puppy to love.

At two, as Alex snoozed on the sofa still in her pj's, someone knocked on the door.

"It's open!"

Auntie M, looking like a small, gray-haired, female Paul Bunyan in a red plaid Pendleton jacket, black watch cap and old jeans tucked into rubber boots, breezed in and marched right to her. "What's the matter, honey?"

"Just enjoying my sabbatical from real life."

Auntie M dropped to the edge of the sofa and put her cold hand on Alex's forehead. "No fever."

"I'm fine. As I said, I'm taking it easy."

"You can talk to me." Swiping off her watch

cap, Auntie M dropped it on the coffee table. "You know that."

"I do know that. It's one of the multitude of things I love about you."

Her aunt bent close and peered at her through squinted eyes. She smelled of hay. She'd probably been out at the horse barn or maybe the rescue barn where Josie currently housed an ancient mule and a family of goats. "You can tell me anything."

"I realize that. But since I'm fine, there's nothing to tell."

"How about some coffee?"

"You want some?" Alex sat up. "I'll—"

"No, no." Auntie M gently pushed her back down. "Stay right there." Auntie M rose and tucked the sofa quilt in around her more securely. "I'm completely capable of making us coffee—or tea? That sounds good, too."

"Tea sounds perfect."

So Auntie M hung up her Pendleton and made them tea. As the tea was brewing, Josie appeared. The three of them sat at the table with their cups of Earl Grey and a box of shortbread cookies Alex had bought when she stocked up the pantry. She told them that she'd marked the pet adoption on her calendar.

"You're getting a pet?" Josie seemed mildly stunned.

"Well, yeah."

Josie blinked at her. "I've just never seen you as someone with a pet."

"I'm not the walk-out-on-your-job-because-of-a-fortune-cookie type, either." She made a face at Auntie M. "*Or* the lie-around-all-day-in-your-reindeer-pajamas type, for that matter." She sat back and pointed at herself with both thumbs. "But look at me now."

Josie squinted at her, just as Auntie M had done back there on the sofa. "Are you okay?"

"Fabulous," she replied much too enthusiastically.

Her sister and her aunt exchanged worried glances. Auntie M said gently, "So much has been going on. We haven't spent enough time together."

Alex waved her hand in front of her face. "Don't be silly. There's been at least one family event per day since I got here."

Josie caught Alex's waving hand, laced their fingers together and gave her a nice, loving squeeze. "Ax," Josie said, using the name she used to call Alex back when Josie toddled around in diapers just learning to talk. "Come to dinner at our house tonight." Josie smiled at their aunt. "Auntie M and Ernesto are coming, too."

"Love to," said Alex, with a big smile—though a tiny part of her wouldn't have minded whiling away the evening lying around in her pajamas thinking about having sex with West.

He was just that good at it.

Come to think of it, West was good at a lot of things—including distracting her from the rudderless dinghy that had somehow become her life. She should have appreciated him more while he was here.

That night at the Halstead house, Alex got to hold Davy, who immediately filled his diaper with a serious load. Hazel jumped up and whisked him away.

"Hey!" Alex called to Hazel's retreating back. "I diapered your stepmom, you know." Or maybe she hadn't. She and Josie were only two years apart. "And if I didn't, I definitely changed the diapers of your aunt Payton..."

"I've got it, Aunt Alex," Hazel called over her shoulder and disappeared down the short hallway that led to the baby's room.

"Everybody loves Davy," said Ash with a nonchalant shrug. "We even compete over who gets to change him."

Alex concentrated on enjoying the evening. Josie made a mean pot roast and Alex really loved seeing how happy her middle sister was with Miles, the girls and the baby. After dinner, they played Monopoly. That went on forever.

They were finally wrapping up when her phone buzzed with a text. She took it out way too eagerly, thinking it might be West—and then remembered that she'd never even gotten his number.

How could that be? She'd shared the cottage with him, spent a spectacular night in bed with the guy—two, counting the night of her sister's wedding last January—and yet somehow, they'd never thought to exchange numbers.

She glanced at the screen and saw it was someone she'd worked with at KJ&T, one of the associates. As she put the phone back in her pocket, she saw that Auntie M was watching her.

"Everything okay?" her aunt asked.

"Good, yeah. Just a friend checking in. I'll get back to her later..."

The wind was up and snow was falling when she rode back to Wild Rose with Ernesto and Auntie M.

Inside the guest cottage, she turned on the fireplace, put her Christmas pajamas on and texted back her former colleague, Rita Sevigny.

Hey. Happy slightly late Thanksgiving...

Alex! I was out last week. Just heard today that you left KJ&T. Talk?

She wasn't close to Rita, but she liked her well enough. She hit the phone icon and Rita picked up. They talked for half an hour. Rita just couldn't believe she'd walked out like that—and on the verge of making partner, too.

Alex said only nice things about KJ&T and everybody who worked there. She'd already burned her bridges, no need to talk trash on top of taking a blowtorch to her career. Before she said goodbye, she and Rita promised to get together for drinks after Christmas.

Would they, really?

Alex doubted it. Somehow, her life in Portland seemed a million miles away, like a dream now, hazy and unreal.

She stayed up till midnight streaming *Bridgerton*. When she went to bed, she couldn't sleep, so she read several chapters of Payton's second published novel. At 3:00 a.m., when she finally turned out the light, she was feeling more than a little disgusted with herself. Insomnia was a bad look on her, especially considering that she had nothing to stay awake stewing about. Her life was smooth sailing, all systems go.

Tuesday was pretty much a repeat of Monday, though she made herself get dressed before she sat around streaming Ali Wong comedy specials and eating candy canes off the tree. She reasoned that as long as she was dressed, if her sister or her aunt dropped by, she wouldn't look like a total slacker.

That day, she got two calls from Portland—one from a casual friend and another from a client who couldn't believe she'd left without reaching out. She chatted with the friend about how she was taking it easy over the holidays. As for the client, she offered confident reassurances that KJ&T would do right by him. During both calls, she kept thinking how far away her old life seemed now. It really hadn't been that long since she'd walked out on the job. It only felt like years and years.

Dinner that night was at Auntie M's. Her sister and her aunt watched her too closely all through the meal and afterward, too.

That night, she promised herself she would go to bed early and get up at seven. She kept that promise.

In the morning, after a quick breakfast, she put on a flannel shirt, overalls, the canvas coat she'd had since her junior year at Heartwood High, her old lace-up work boots and a knit hat. Out in the horse barn, she found Clark Stockwell, who had been working at Wild Rose since right after Davy's birth.

"Hey, Clark," she said, bending to pet his sweet dog, Big Nose. "Put me to work."

Clark looked mildly surprised that the lawyer

from Portland suddenly couldn't wait to muck stalls and feed stock. But he didn't argue. She worked the entire morning. Around noon, she looked up from grooming one of the twins' ponies to see her aunt striding toward her.

"Lunch at my cottage," said Auntie M. "Twelve thirty?"

The pony, Deke, snorted and flicked his tail as Alex brushed his flank. "You don't need to invite me for every meal, you know."

"Yes, I do. I'm leaving tomorrow." She and Ernesto were heading back to Salinas for a couple of weeks. They would return before Christmas. "Right now, I want every minute I can get with you."

What could she say to that? "Same." They shared a smile. "Twelve thirty. I'll be there."

She quickly finished grooming Deke and returned to the guest cottage for a quick shower. Josie's Jeep was parked at Auntie M's when Alex headed over there.

The minute she walked in the door Alex knew something was up. From the threshold, she could see straight through to the kitchen. Her aunt and her sister stood at the sink, side by side. They both had that look—like the sound of the door opening had interrupted a discussion, something they didn't want her to hear.

She pretended she hadn't noticed anything.

Why push it? They would say more than she ever wanted to hear when they were damn good and ready.

They waited until midway through lunch before starting in on her.

Auntie M took the lead, announcing that she'd decided to stick around until after Christmas. Ernesto would return to Salinas alone.

Alex set down her fork with a bite of pasta salad still on it. "You know you want to be with him. And he wants to be with you. Don't you even waste a minute. Go to Salinas. Come back at Christmas as planned. You won't be missing a thing here, I promise you."

Josie spoke up then. "Alex, she's worried about you—I'm worried, too."

"Not the worry card." Alex pushed her plate away. "Please. No, I'm not the most fun anyone ever had lately. But really. I'm doing all right, I really am. I'm getting by, you know, figuring things out..."

Auntie M wasn't convinced. "You seem downhearted. Especially in the last few days."

How did they know these things? And if she had to say *I'm fine* one more time, she just might leap to her feet and run out the door screaming. "I'm managing. I am."

"Did something go wrong Sunday?" asked

Josie. "Since then, you really seem like you're feeling low."

Alex glared at her sister. "You don't want to know."

"Yes, we do," they said in unison. It was scary how well her family knew her.

"You keep after me, I'm just going to tell you."

They only stared at her, waiting. By then, they knew she would give it up. And they were right.

"Okay, it's like this. You remember my fortune—the one I taped to an index card?"

"Do it now." Josie put her hand against her heart. "How could we forget?"

Auntie M was ready with the real question. "What, exactly, did you *do*?"

"Weston," she said, and watched their mouths fall open in unison. "I slept with West on Sunday night."

Chapter Seven

"Wait!" Josie required clarification. "You're saying you had sex with Weston?"

Alex slapped both hands over her mouth and muttered through her fingers, "Could you please just forget I said that?"

"No," her aunt and her sister replied in unison.

Josie added, "You did say it. Admit it."

Reluctantly, she nodded. "Yes, after the wedding Sunday night, I had sex with Weston."

Her sister and her aunt turned their heads in unison—to gape at each other this time. When they looked at Alex again, Josie said, "Well. Um. Good for you."

"And good for Weston," said Auntie M with a

determined nod. "He's a lucky man to get a chance with you."

"You two seemed to get along great together," added Josie, sounding both insistent and weirdly uneasy.

Alex glanced from her sister to her aunt and back to her sister again. "I love you guys—but you really have no idea what you're talking about."

"Okay..." Josie spoke more cautiously now. "So tell us. Bring us up to speed."

Alex chewed on the corner of her lip as she tried to decide how much to say. Should she mention what had happened on Payton and Easton's wedding night last January? Probably not. That had been a rough night for West, which made it a story for him to tell, not her. "Well, it's not a relationship or anything..." Ugh. That sounded awful in the wimpiest possible way. "What I mean is, West and I, we do have a connection, I guess you could say. Wc likc cach othcr, wc do, but..." Dropping her head back, she groaned at the ceiling. "I should never have said anything."

Chair legs scraped the floor as her aunt and her sister jumped up at the same time.

"Yes, you should!" Auntie M bent close and hugged her on one side.

Josie grabbed her on the other. "Whatever you need, that's what we're here for."

Alex slipped one arm around each of them

and squeezed right back. "You guys—this. Right now. With both of you. The love and the acceptance and the understanding. That's what I need. And that's what you give me."

"Oh, baby." Auntie M pressed a kiss to her cheek as Josie hugged her tighter.

Alex allowed herself a minute to bask in all the unconditional love before suggesting, "I know it's only lunchtime, but wine would be good."

Auntie M opened a bottle and they shared it. They laughed together over the vagaries of love and relationships and one-night stands.

Alex confessed, "I really have no idea how to explain this thing with West. I don't really understand it myself."

"And that is o-*kay*!" Josie raised her glass and knocked back a mouthful.

"When you know, you know," announced Auntie M.

Alex laughed. "But I *don't* know. That's what I'm trying to tell you guys."

"And you don't *have* to know," said Josie.

"Do you regret Sunday night?" asked Auntie M.

She realized she might be a tiny bit freaked out about it. But regret it? She didn't. Not in the least. "Nope. Not one bit."

Josie raised her glass. "To great men and excellent sex!"

They all three drank to that.

After which, Josie said, "There is one little thing, though..."

Her tentative tone alerted Alex. "You're about to say something I don't want to hear, aren't you?"

"Well, it's only, what about Payton?"

"What about her?"

"Alex, I really think you need to tell Payton what happened with you and West."

All the happy, wine-drenched feelings drained right out of her. She slid a glance at Auntie M, hoping for support. Though support for what, exactly, she wasn't sure. Auntie M kept her mouth shut—because she was older and wiser and knew when to just sit there and let things play out.

Alex asked Josie, "Why on earth would I do that?"

"Because if you don't, we all three have to keep your secret from our sister. That means Payton will be in the dark and we will know what's going on in this situation that involves you and her brother-in-law and that will drive a wedge between us. And that's not healthy."

"Good point," said Auntie M softly.

Alex closed her eyes. She breathed slow and deep. "Yep. I never should have told you two."

"But you did," replied Josie. "And you needed to. And now you need to tell our sister, as well."

"You know she's going to turn right around and tell Easton." When Josie winced, Alex pressed her point. "And that could go poorly in so many ways."

"It's better to be honest and you know that, Alex. You just need to put it right out there and work through the blowback."

"You can say that when *you've* slept with your sister's husband's brother."

"Okay, when you put it that way, you make sleeping with West sound slightly...reprehensible."

"Ya think?"

"Alex, what I'm getting at is that it's just in your mind. Why shouldn't you spend a night with West? Why shouldn't he have a night with you? He's single. You're single. There is nothing at all wrong with what happened between you."

"Great. There's nothing wrong with it. So why does my baby sister *have* to know about it?"

Josie just looked at her, pleading with those big amber eyes of hers. Auntie M was no better, all the stuff she hadn't said was right there on her face. Auntie M agreed with Josie, but no way would she speak up and make it two against one.

"All right." Alex slid her phone from the thigh pocket of her leggings. "I'll text her."

Josie just looked at her.

Alex surrendered. "Fine. Not the kind of information that should be delivered via text. Calling Payton right now." She brought up Payton's contact and hit the call icon as Josie mouthed, *Thank you.*

Payton answered on the first ring. "Hi. What?"

Alex knew that tone of voice. "You're writing. I'll call back later."

"No. Work can wait. Talk to me."

Alex glanced from Josie to her aunt. They both stared at her through wide eyes. "I'm just going to say it. I slept with Weston on Sunday night."

There was a moment of echoing silence. Finally, Payton asked, "Did you have a good time with him?"

Alex smiled. What had she been worried about? Payton never had been the least bit judgmental about relationships or sex. "I had a great time, yes. I like West. We had lots of fun—at the wedding and then for the rest of the night."

"Do you regret having sex with him?"

Her answer hadn't changed since Auntie M asked her earlier. "No. I don't regret it."

"But it's been on your mind?"

"Yes. Yes, it has."

"And you felt you just had to tell me about it today for some reason?"

"No. I needed to talk about it."

"Okay, yeah. That makes sense. So you called me."

"Not exactly. I told Auntie M and Josie and

they said I had to tell you or we would all be keeping it from you and that would be wrong."

"They're standing right there, staring at you, aren't they?"

"Yes, they are."

"Put me on speaker."

Alex hit the speaker icon. "You're on speaker—and, Payton, I'm really hoping that you don't feel you *have* to tell Easton. This is just getting too strange and I can't believe I didn't keep it to myself."

"Oh, come on," said Payton.

"Yeah," Josie spoke up. "Who else would you tell?"

Auntie M was nodding. "We're here for you. We love you."

"And I love you—but, Payton, do you *have* to tell Easton?"

Payton took too long to answer. "I'm sorry, Alex. But yeah. I kind of do. It may sound self-righteous, but honesty is everything with Easton and me."

Alex blew out a slow, resigned breath. "Not self-righteous at all. And I kind of figured you'd say that." She glared at Josie, who at least had the grace to look sheepish.

"But don't worry," Payton said. "Easton will be fine with it."

"You're sure about that?"

"Well, *I'm* fine with it."

"Yeah, but, Payton, you're not a guy."

"Isn't that maybe just a little bit sexist?"

Josie let out a snort of laughter. "Yeah, and maybe also just a little bit true."

"Josie," Payton said sternly. "Easton is not going to overreact. Alex, you and Weston have done nothing wrong. And I will make certain that Easton understands and accepts that you've done nothing wrong and what two consenting adults do in private is nobody else's business. You'll see. Easton will be fine about this."

"I hope you're right."

"I know my own husband." Payton sounded so confident.

Alex tried to take comfort in that. "One more thing. Joyce and Myron. Please don't tell me *they* have to know, too."

Payton didn't even pause to think about it. "Forget that. They never need to know. I mean, honesty matters, but telling Joyce and Myron is a bridge too far."

"Well, that's something at least."

"It's all going to work out great, you'll see."

Back at the guest cottage an hour later, Alex paced the floor.

She wanted to believe Payton, but what if Payton was wrong and Easton reacted badly when he found out about Sunday night? Alex cringed at the thought.

And that had her realizing that West deserved a heads-up.

A moment later, she remembered that she didn't have his number.

For a good ten minutes, she vacillated—sit back and let it play out? Or find a way to let the guy know that she'd opened her big mouth?

Somehow, not having his number made the situation even worse. Really? How could she have spent two spectacular nights in bed with him and never thought to get a number?

Finally, Alex texted her aunt. I think I should warn West that Payton is telling Easton we slept together. Do you have Weston's number?

Auntie M had an actual spiral-bound address book. And she had everybody's number in more ways than one. The phone rang in Alex's hand.

Alex answered with, "No, West and I did not exchange numbers."

Auntie M asked gently, "Sweetie, do you want me to come over there?"

"Thank you and I love you, but no. What I need is to call West so he knows what's going on."

"Hold on." Thirty seconds later, Auntie M rattled off the number. As Alex entered it into her phone, her aunt asked, "You sure you're all right, Alexandra?"

"I am, yes." Total lie. But she'd set this crap in motion and she wasn't going to start whining about it now.

"I'm here if you need me," said Auntie M. "Right now or anytime. Just say the word."

"I know. And you always have been and I can't tell you how much that means to me." She said goodbye and called West before she could chicken out.

He didn't pick up. No surprise. Even if he *wanted* to hear from her, he wouldn't recognize the number. She should have texted.

But it had already gone to voice mail. "This is Weston. Leave a message." She smiled like a doofus at the sound of his recorded voice and it took her a minute after the beep to start talking.

When she hung up, she tossed the phone down on the coffee table, pressed her hands to her flaming-hot cheeks and wondered what could have possessed her to imagine it would be a good idea to tell her aunt and Josie that she'd had sex with West.

Weston sat at his desk at Wright Hospitality crunching the numbers for a potential acquisition—a small resort in Palm Springs called Tres Palmas—when his cell lit up.

He glanced at the screen. Voice mail. Probably a spam call. He went ahead and checked it anyway.

"Hi, West. It's Alex." The sound of her voice had him wishing it were still Sunday night. She rattled off a number. "Would you give me a call, please, as soon as you get a chance? We need to talk. We've got a little family issue you should know about."

Alex. With a *family issue*?

Wary, intrigued—and ridiculously pleased that she'd reached out whatever the reason—he rose from his desk and went to the window. He stared out on Puget Sound as he called Alex back.

"Hello, Weston." The weary tone of her voice did not reassure him.

"You okay?"

"I'm just going to say it." She swiftly explained that her sisters and her aunt Marilyn now knew where he'd spent Sunday night. According to her, none of them had a problem with that. "Payton insisted she has to tell Easton. She swears that your brother won't be bothering you about it."

"Of course she does."

"My thoughts exactly." Gingerly, she suggested, "There's good news, too."

"So glad to hear that."

"The three of us agreed that your parents never have to know."

"Well, that's something, at least." He should leave the past out of this. But he had to know. "What about East and Payton's wedding night last January? Did you tell them about that, too?"

"No! I didn't. That's different."

Remembering that night pressed on a tender spot down inside him. "Different, how?"

"Just not my story to tell, I guess."

Damn. He really did like this woman. A lot. "Thank you."

"West, I really am sorry that I told them about Sunday. I'm not sure why I didn't just keep my mouth shut."

Someone rapped on his office door. "Hold on a second, would you?"

"Of course."

The phone still at his ear, he turned from the window, strode to the door and pulled it wide. His brother stood on the other side looking ready to kick some ass. "East. That was quick."

Down on the farm, Alex moaned, "I knew it."

"I'll call you right back as soon as I handle this situation." He hung up.

His brother stepped forward, grabbed the door and shut it harder than necessary behind him. "What the hell are you doing, sleeping with Alex?"

West frowned as he considered that question. And the more he considered, the more this whole thing pissed him the hell off. "You know, East. It's really not your business what Alex and I do in private. We're both single. No one is waiting at home for either of us."

He realized his frown had morphed into a grin when Easton demanded, "What are you smiling about?"

"It just occurred to me that you've got no damn room to talk." Before East could lay down a lecture, West went on, "Aren't you the guy who had a fling with Payton and then failed to get her number *or* her last name, which meant that years went by before you finally found her again and learned you had twin sons?"

Both of Easton's hands curled to fists at his sides. He didn't throw a punch, but he wanted to. Bad.

West almost felt sorry for him. "All right. That was uncalled-for. I know that was a tough five years for you—and for Payton. And as for your burning need to punch me out..." He spread his arms wide. "If it will make you feel better, take your shot."

East scowled. "I can't."

West guessed, "Because Payton made you promise not to?"

"Don't give me that smirk."

West shook his head. "I can't help it. You should see your face."

"What were you thinking? Just tell me that."

"What do you want from me? I like Alex. She likes me. We're not hurting anybody. We're both responsible adults. There is no reason we can't do whatever we damn well please together."

"West. Wake the hell up. You mess around with her and then you get bored and she gets hurt and we all pay the price because there's trouble in the family."

"You don't know that's what'll happen."

"I know that you're not interested in anything serious with a woman. And I know that Alex has issues right now. She's trying to figure out what to do with the rest of her life. You won't help her if you go making things even more complicated for her than they already are."

Was that true? Was he a bad influence? Or did he offer just what she needed right now—someone to laugh with, someone to hold, someone to lighten things up when she might be feeling down? Not everything went on forever. Sometimes you just had to reach out and grab on to a good thing for as long as it lasted.

He could hear her husky voice in his head. *And here I was hoping for a Christmas affair...*

He wanted that. He wanted it bad—the two of them, together, doing whatever the hell they felt like doing. He wanted *her*, wanted to take her up on her offer, wanted her in his arms every night till the New Year. Why shouldn't they have what they both wanted?

East said, "I don't like that look on your face."

"Too bad."

"Just tell me you'll leave her alone from now on."

"I think you're over the line here, my brother. Alex and I, we're the ones who'll decide about that."

Alex sat on the sofa with her phone in one hand and a vodka tonic in the other. The phone rang. West. She answered before it could ring a second time. "Hi. Be honest. Is everything okay?"

"More or less. East really wanted to punch me in the face, but Payton made him promise not to."

"I don't believe this is happening." She knocked back a big sip of her drink.

"I hear ice cubes rattling. You broke out the scotch."

"Vodka, but yeah. Drowning my sorrows. Swimming in liquor and regret. Beating myself up for opening my big fat mouth."

He chuckled, the sound sexy and deep. "It's not that bad. Nothing happened with East. He and I just cleared the air."

"What does that even mean?"

"It means everything's okay up here in Seattle and you need to stop being so hard on yourself."

"Humph."

"Alex. Tell me the truth. Are you okay?"

"I am, yeah. I'm just not all that thrilled that everyone knows what we were up to Sunday night—even if I am the one who opened her big fat mouth about it."

"Hey. I meant what I just said. Everything's fine here."

"Please. Your brother wanted to put his fist through your face."

"Like that hasn't happened before—but there's a bright side. He didn't. And he's not going to. It's all good." He teased, "You should watch the day drinking, though. That can be a slippery slope."

She raised her glass to him, even though it wasn't a video call and he couldn't see her do it. "I promise I'll only have this one."

"All right, then. I'm holding you to it." She thought how happy she was to hear his voice again. And then he asked, "You sure you're okay?"

She pressed the cold glass to her suddenly hot cheek. "More or less. I'm not sure why I told Josie and Auntie M about us. Honestly, I've never been someone who can't keep her business to herself. But we were talking, me and Josie and Auntie M, and… I don't know. I just went ahead and told them." She set the half-full drink on the coffee table and stared at the tree in the window.

"Alex, are you sorry about Sunday night?"

"No! West, I'm not. It was a great night."

"Damn right it was." His voice had gone deliciously rough. "And that stuff I said when I was leaving, I apologize for that. I didn't know what to say. I opened my mouth and a bunch of garbage came out."

"There's no need to apologize. You felt what you felt—just like I felt a little let down that you were leaving."

"Yeah?" The question rubbed all her nerve endings in a really lovely way.

"Yeah. West, I had this feeling…"

"Tell me."

"You don't need to hear this. You really don't. I shouldn't have told them. It only made trouble between you and Easton."

"He'll get over it. And sometimes honesty really is the best way to go."

"Yeah. I'll tell myself that, why not?"

"And while you're at it, tell *me* about this *feeling* you had."

She wished she hadn't promised herself not to have a second drink. "We probably shouldn't go there."

"Alex. We're going there. You know that we are."

She had shivers down her arms—and that fluttery feeling in her belly. "What are you saying?"

"I'm saying that Sunday night flat-out wasn't enough."

"Oh." It came out soft. Breathless.

"Miss me?" he asked. "At least a little?"

"Maybe a tiny bit. I definitely felt let down when you left."

"Because this thing with us, it's not done yet."

"You feel that way, too?"

"Didn't I just say that Sunday night wasn't enough?"

"Yeah. You did…"

There was a beep on his end of the line. "Hold on. I've got to see what this is."

"I should just let you—"

"Don't go anywhere, Alex. I'll be half a minute, tops." He was as good as his word. Thirty seconds later, he said, "Hey. I do have to go. It's one of those work calls I have to take…"

She reminded herself that she did not feel disappointed he had to hang up, not in the least. "That's all right. See you at Christmas, West."

"Yes, you will. I can't wait."

West wrapped up his call and went back to working on the numbers for Tres Palmas. At three, he met with the top people in accounting and then with the head of HR.

But his mind wasn't on the job.

He wanted to see Alex.

And he didn't want to wait till Christmas. He wasn't the patient one—that was East.

Back when they were growing up, East would

never sneak a peek under the tree. When Christmas morning came, every present with his name on it looked spanking fresh and festive, no rips in the pretty paper, every ribbon shiny and new, tied just so.

West's presents? They always looked like some little mouse had chewed on them, the tape pulled away from the paper, a hole or two in the wrapping at the corners, the ribbons all tattered and torn.

His mother would sigh and his dad would lecture him.

Then the next year, he would do it all over again. He never could wait till Christmas morning to find out what he was getting.

He felt that way about Alex right now.

Only more so. Because he already knew exactly what he would be getting—and he could not wait to get it again. She'd offered him Christmastime. Why shouldn't he reach out with both hands and take it?

By five, he'd made up his mind.

East stuck his head in at five thirty. "We good?" West looked up from his desk—and Easton knew. He stepped all the way into the office and shut the door. "You're going back down to Wild Rose, aren't you?"

West shut his laptop. "You know I've got vacation days piled up. The holidays are a good time to use them. I'll put in a couple of all-nighters to make sure everything's caught up and I'll drive down Saturday, stay until New Year's. Whatever absolutely has to get done here in the next month, I can deal with remotely. I'll fly back and forth for any meetings I can't miss."

"You're giving me your itinerary?" demanded Easton. "That's not what I'm talking about." East dropped to the leather sofa on the south wall, raked both hands back through his hair—and then popped up to his feet again. He paced the floor. "I don't believe this. I can't even beat the crap out of you right now. Payton made me promise not to throw a single punch." He stopped in front of Weston's desk. "Let's go to Oliver's." The famous bar was located nearby, in the lobby of the Mayflower Park Hotel. "We'll talk."

"I'm not going to change my mind, East."

They went to Oliver's anyway. The drinks were great. Easton pulled out all the stops. West held firm.

That night at his place, he called Alex.

"West." She sounded happy to hear his voice. "What's going on?"

They talked for an hour.

He knew he should tell her that he planned to drive down to the farm early Saturday morning—and stay right there in the cottage with her until the New Year.

But he wanted to surprise her. And he wanted to be there, right in front of her, to see the look in her face when he showed up.

Alex had no trouble saying what she wanted. If she wanted him gone, he'd just turn around and come home.

Yeah, it did occur to him that East would tell Payton of his plans and Payton would tell her sister. So what? He still hoped he might get to surprise Alex, to watch her reaction when he breezed in the cottage door.

Thursday night, he worked until eight. He called Alex during the drive home.

She told him that her aunt Marilyn and Ernesto had left that day for Salinas.

"So," he said. "Now it's just you, alone, at Wild Rose Farm?"

"No, I am not alone. Clark Stockwell and his sweet dog, Big Nose, are here. And Josie and Miles are right next door. I had dinner over there tonight."

"So you're not feeling lonely, then?"

"Nope. I reached out to an old high school friend. We're meeting for happy hour at a place she likes in Hood River tomorrow night."

Again, he considered breaking the news of his upcoming visit. But he didn't. And it was clear that she had no idea he would be driving down. For whatever reason, Payton hadn't told her.

Maybe East hadn't told Payton because he still hoped he could talk West out of going—or maybe his brother and his sister-in-law had finally decided to butt the hell out and let him and Alex run their own lives for a change.

That would be refreshing.

Alex called *him* Friday night. Her name popped up on his phone and he grinned like a fool.

He swiped up. "Missed me, huh?"

"I think I've grown accustomed to hearing your voice."

"How was happy hour with your old school friend?"

"Good. We caught up. She's got a six-year-old little girl and a ten-year-old son and she's super active in the PTA."

"So you two have a lot in common, huh?"

"Don't be a smart-ass, West."

"You knew I was trouble when you said I could stay in the back bedroom."

"But that's just the thing—you *didn't* stay in the back bedroom, did you?"

He almost told her right then.

But no. The surprise would be too much fun.

"West? You still there?"

"Where else would I be?"

"I don't know, I think I always pictured you living the fancy bachelor life, partying at some exclusive club where you have to be a member and there's a sex dungeon in the basement."

"I really hate to disappoint you, but I'm still at the office."

She chided, "West, it's after eight."

"I've got a few things to wrap up."

"And *then* you'll party all night?"

"Nah. I'll head home. Get a good night's sleep." *Get on the road early tomorrow.*

"*Now* you tell me you're just an ordinary, everyday workaholic. All my illusions are officially shattered."

"Don't worry about me. I know how to have fun."

"Yes." She said it softly. "Yes, you do."

He wanted to say he missed her, that he couldn't wait to see her.

But he was afraid he would give himself away.

They talked about nothing in particular for another ten minutes and then said good-night.

The next morning, he was on the road before dawn. He got to the farm at a little after ten.

A light snow was falling, the wind blowing the white flakes around every which way. In the front window of the guest cottage, the tree lights shone bright. Leaving his luggage in his Range Rover to deal with later, he got out. The snow crunched under his boots as he ran up the front steps.

From inside, he heard what he guessed was Michael Bublé singing "It's Beginning to Look a Lot Like Christmas." That made him grin. Alex must be in a holiday mood. He raised his hand to ring the doorbell—and then checked the door handle instead.

It was open.

And he shouldn't.

He knew it.

But he'd never been the good twin. He'd always loved to misbehave—to put salt in the sugar bowl, to jump out from behind the furniture and shout, "Boo!" when his mother was dusting the living room.

Slowly, he turned the handle and pushed the door inward. Michael Bublé crooned all the louder. A wave of warm, sweet-smelling air came out and wrapped around him.

Cookies. She must be baking cookies. He hadn't realized Alex baked. There were far too many things he didn't know about her.

She stood on the other side of the kitchen island with her back to him, wearing a red sweater, all that thick dark hair piled on her head in a flyaway bun. Damn, she looked fine. He wanted to grab her and help her out of that red sweater.

Maybe he would get lucky and she would want the same thing. Only one way to find out.

He stepped into the warm, cookie-scented cottage and silently shut the door. It took a few seconds to shed his heavy jacket. He hung it on one of the pegs by the door.

Crossing the living area without making a sound, he rounded the island as she finished arranging cookie-dough shapes on a cookie sheet. She scooped up the baking sheet and turned for the stove. He moved with her, staying behind her.

Tiptoeing up close, he said, "So, Alex, about that Christmas affair you offered me..."

With a startled cry, she whirled on him. Eyes wide, her mouth a shocked O, she sent the sheet of cookies flying.

Chapter Eight

"Weston!" Alex shrieked.

Deftly, he snatched the sheet of unbaked cookies from midair. "Got it!" And he grinned that devilish grin of his. "Christmas cookies. My favorite!"

She whacked him on the arm with the back of her hand. He deserved it for sneaking up on her like that—even if she was wildly happy to see him. "You scared ten years off my life!"

He had a look full of delicious bad intentions. They stared at each other over the cookie-dough candy canes, Santas and snowmen. He asked, "Well?"

"Um. Was there a question?"

"Our Christmas affair. Yes or no?"

She made a thoughtful little sound.

He tugged on a wave of her hair that had escaped her messy bun, brushing the side of her cheek as he did it, sending a cascade of sweet sensation tumbling through her. "Yes or no?"

She bit the inside of her lip to keep from smiling too wide. "Yes."

His gaze ran over her, a leisurely look that was every bit as thrilling as any actual caress. "So you're saying I can stay here with you till New Year's?"

She took the cookie sheet from him, turned, pulled the oven open, slid the sheet onto the rack and shut the oven door. Breathing slow and even to settle her racing heart, she faced him again. "Don't you have to work?"

"I will work. Remotely—and I'll probably have to fly to Seattle a time or two."

"So Easton knows you're here?"

"He does."

"The family—"

"I have a suggestion." His crooked smile lit her up inside.

"Oh, I'm sure you do." She tried to sound stern. Total fail.

"Let's talk about all this later." He closed the small distance between them, bent close and ran his nose up the side of her neck. Every nerve in her body danced. "You smell like sugar and vanilla."

"It's the cookies."

"Yum." His teeth grazed her throat. "I could eat you right up."

She lifted her arms, braced them on his shoulders and sighed as he nipped and sucked his way up over her chin to her parted mouth.

"Now we're getting somewhere." His lips met hers and his long, warm fingers curled around the back of her neck. "Alex…" He growled her name into her mouth. "You *taste* like sugar, too."

With a moan, she pressed her whole body against him as his hand strayed upward into her hair. "You should definitely stay with me till New Year's."

"Done." He tugged on her topknot and it came tumbling down.

Still kissing her, he walked her backward. They rounded the end of the island closest to the oven and kept on going. The kiss went on, too, as he backed her the length of the main room, into the tiny square of hallway and through her open bedroom door.

When they got to the bed, he started undressing her. She was naked in two minutes flat. How convenient that she hadn't made the bed yet. She fell back across the sheets as he stripped off his own clothes.

In no time he was wearing nothing at all. He was such a good-looking man, lean, cut and strong—and every bit as glad to see her as she was to have him here. She knew that from the hot gleam in his eyes and that wonderful, crooked smile of his. Plus, there was no way to ignore that impressive erection.

Joining her on the bed, he planted his knees on either side of her hip bones and his hands on either side of her head. "Yes, I am very glad to see you."

"How did you know that's what I was thinking?"

"The way you look at me."

"I'm that obvious?"

"You might have licked your lips once or twice."

She laughed. "Bust-ed. And you're right." She trailed a slow finger down the center of his sculpted chest. "I really am glad to see you."

He dropped a quick, hard kiss on her mouth. "Condoms?"

"Bedside drawer where you left them."

He reached over, pulled the drawer open and took out a few, dropping them within easy reach. "Alex. It's so good to see you—*all* of you. Every. Gorgeous. Inch." He kissed those last three words onto her lips.

She grabbed him close, the breath fleeing her chest as she took his weight and heat and hardness all along the front of her. She kissed him so deep, learning the tender contours of his lips all over again.

He laughed, low and rough. The sound echoed in her head as she rolled them, gaining the top position, pulling away just long enough to slide down his body, bend over him—and take him in her mouth.

"Alex..." He groaned her name like a plea, reaching down, framing her head between his hands, holding on as she took him deep, then gathering her hair, getting it out of the way so that he could see exactly what she did to him.

Twice, he tried to pull away, growling deep in his throat, warning, "I won't last," and then, "I can't hold out..."

She hummed low and stayed on task. From the main room, Pentatonix sang "Hallelujah."

"Alex. It's happening," he warned. "It's happening right now!"

She hummed around him, staying with him as he came.

When she finally let him go, he caught her by the shoulders and pulled her up his body so their lips could meet. "I think I might have died. Am I in heaven?"

"Could be." She rolled off him and onto her pillow with a happy sigh.

He turned his head and frowned at her. "Do you smell smoke?"

She snickered. "So then, maybe not heaven, after all?" Right then, the smoke alarm started screaming. That had her shouting, "My cookies!" Bolting upright and jumping from the bed, she raced for the kitchen, West close on her heels.

In the kitchen, the smoke was thick near the ceiling and the alarm continued to blare. Alex grabbed a pot holder and pulled open the oven. A cloud of smoke rolled out. She seized the baking sheet of charred cookies and dropped it on the cooktop, then turned off the oven. West opened the window over the sink. Cold, snow-damp air blew in on the wind.

They fanned at the smoke with their hands, coughing and laughing. By the time enough of it had vanished out the window that the alarm stopped, she was shivering—which was not the least surprising. Both of them were stark naked and the icy wind outside was fierce.

West shut the window. In the living area, she turned on the fireplace, set the furnace fan to run continuously until the smoke had completely cleared out and instructed her Google Assistant to turn off the music.

He came up behind her, clasped her bare waist between his hands and whispered in her ear, "Let's warm you up." Scooping her high against his chest, he carried her back to her bed and wrapped the covers around them both.

Soon she was toasty warm.

They started kissing again.

In no time, he was reaching for a condom. She took it from him, rolled it down over him and pulled him on top of her. It felt so good with him, so right…

Right for right now, she reminded herself as they moved together. She needed to reinvent her life. No way was she ready for anything serious—and he'd made it way clear that he wasn't, either.

Still, with him, she felt special, important and so womanly, somehow. He behaved as if he couldn't get enough of her, like he just couldn't wait to get close to her again. She felt the same about him—and not only because of the great sex. She also loved laughing with him, hanging out with him. She could talk to him about pretty much anything.

"I'm sorry your cookies are ruined," he whispered a little later as they snuggled together under the covers.

She kissed the edge of his chiseled jaw. "Not a big deal. That was the last cookie sheetful. The others came out okay."

He skated a finger down the bridge of her nose. "Just okay?"

"West. The truth is, I never was much of a

baker. I just got in the mood for Christmas cookies today."

He nuzzled her ear. "I'll munch your cookies any day."

She snort-laughed at that one and when he tried to kiss her, she pressed her hands against his chest and held his gaze. "You know we need to talk about the family." He dipped in close and stole a kiss anyway. She warned, "Don't try to distract me."

He put on a pouty look. "I would never..."

"Back to the main point." She combed the hair at his temples with her fingers. "You said Easton knows you're here with me. What about Payton?"

He lifted his shoulder in a half shrug. "I didn't ask, so I have no idea what your sister knows."

"Your parents?"

"I don't know for certain, but it's doubtful. I can't see my brother or your sister telling them. Too weird and awkward."

"But they will know in two weeks when they show up for Christmas."

"How about we look at it this way? There's no reason to start explaining as long as they don't ask. You never know. They might just stay on their own side of the fence."

"Well, we can hope—and Josie invited me to her house for dinner tonight."

He pulled her closer, caught her lower lip between his teeth and worried it lightly. "Do I get to go with you?"

"Of course."

"Whew. I don't like picturing myself sitting here alone waiting for Uber Eats to bring me my takeout."

"I want you to come. You should know, though, that me and my sisters tell one another everything. So I'm going to call Josie first, to let her know that you're staying with me until New Year's. I'll say I would like to bring you with me to dinner. I'll also be calling Payton to let her know what's going on."

"Great," he said, in a voice that implied it was anything but.

"You have objections?"

"No way. They're your sisters."

"Right answer." She sat up and pushed the covers down.

He snaked a hard arm around her and pulled her back against him. "You don't need to call them right this minute, do you?"

"There's no reason to put it off."

He caught her earlobe between his teeth and bit it lightly, causing lovely, fluttery sensations all through her body. "This bed is warm and you're so soft and smooth..."

She did love that hungry look in his eye. It

caused a hot, heavy feeling low in her belly. "We can't stay in bed forever. After I call my sisters, I need to go get a puppy."

His golden eyebrows drew together. "You really are getting a puppy?"

"I am."

"And for some reason, it has to be today?"

"Yes. It's Clear the Shelter Saturday at Heartwood Animal Rescue. I'm going. And that's why I do need to get moving."

He pulled her closer. "No problem. I'll make this quick..."

An hour later, Alex had showered and dressed. West was taking his turn in the bathroom.

She called Josie first. "Got a minute?"

"For you? Always."

"I'm just going to put it right out there. West is here. He's staying with me until New Year's."

"Wow..." Josie let the word trail off.

Alex answered the questions her sister hadn't even asked yet. "I like him, Josie. He showed up a couple of hours ago. I'm really happy he's here."

"Well, okay, then. Bring him to dinner tonight."

"Thanks. I will."

"So..." Josie let the single word trail off significantly.

"Go ahead. Ask me."

"It's serious, then?"

"It's a fling, Josephine."

Josie didn't ask, *Are you sure about this?* But the question hung in the silence between them. "I'm here. To talk. To listen. Whatever you need."

"Thank you. I love you."

"And I love you."

"Guess what? West and I are heading to Heartwood Animal Rescue today. I'm getting a puppy."

"Terrific. Bring your puppy to dinner, too."

"Thanks for the offer. We'll see how it goes."

As soon as she hung up with Josie, she texted Payton. We should talk. Not an emergency. Just, you know, when you get a minute.

Payton didn't immediately reply, so Alex straightened up the kitchen. She washed the bowl and utensils, scraped burned cookies into the compost bin, put the cookie sheet in the sink to soak and wiped down the counters. As she was drying the mixing bowl, her phone pinged with a text.

It was Payton. I can guess what you want to talk about. Did Weston arrive safely? Call me.

Alex put away the bowl and made the call. When Payton picked up, Alex asked, "So Easton told you everything, huh?"

"Of course. And I am carefully minding my own damn business."

"Thank you for that."

"You're welcome. Having fun?"

"You're givin' me lip, Paytaytochip?" It was what they all used to call Payton way back in the day—complete with the requisite silly rhyme.

"As the former wild child of this family, I get it. You're amazing. He's charming and hot. There are fireworks, am I right?"

"So very right."

"You should both have a great time."

"We should, yes. And we are, I promise you."

"Also, I've forbidden Easton to beat up his brother, so violence won't be a problem."

"Well, that's a relief."

Payton reminded her to call anytime, same as Josie had. They were saying goodbye as West emerged from the short hallway to the bedrooms. Alex set her phone down as West faced her across the kitchen island.

His hair was a darker shade of gold, still wet from his shower. He gave her that teasing smirk of his, but his eyes held a hint of concern. "Everything okay?"

"You're invited to dinner at Josie's. As for my call to Payton, she already knew you were here."

His smile had reached his eyes as he rounded the island and got up close and personal. "All good, then."

"I would say so, yes." She went into his arms. He smelled like soap and pine trees. Their kiss lit her up, head to toe. Eventually she had to press her hands against his chest to back him off a little. "If you keep doing that, I'll never get my puppy."

He took a keyless car remote from his pocket. "Let's go, then."

"That reminds me. You'll need your key to the cottage." She eased around him to get it from the utility drawer. "Here you go."

Outside, the snow had stopped. The wind had not. It tried to whip their coats right off their bodies. They climbed in his big Range Rover and off they went.

"What kind of puppy are we looking for?" he asked as he turned onto the main road to Heartwood.

"I was thinking a boxer. Or a Labrador retriever. A short-haired breed, medium to large. Bigger dogs have calmer personalities."

He slanted her a quick glance. "Not always."

"Well, I'm thinking I'll know the puppy for me as soon as I see him."

"And your puppy will be a male, short-haired, medium to large?"

She nodded firmly. "That much, I'm sure of." She thought of the last pet she'd had, back when she was growing up here on the farm. Sometimes she still missed Old Betsy.

He seemed to sense her change of mood. "Everything okay?"

"Just thinking that I haven't had a pet since Old Betsy died. Old Betsy was a dwarf goat, a rescue. She used to follow me everywhere. Broke my heart when she died."

He sent her another glance—a sympathetic one this time. "How long ago?"

"Almost twenty years. I was fourteen when I lost her. When she died, I told myself that pets weren't for me. It hurts too much to lose them. And then, well…"

He met her eyes again, just for a moment. They shared a smile and he said, "You've been busy with school, with your job."

"Exactly. And I have no idea what I'm going to do with my life from now on. But whatever I decide is next, I'm not spending all my time at the office. I need a real life. And I think it's time, you know, to have a friend around the house."

West parked his car in the single empty parking space at Heartwood Animal Rescue. The low, square building took up half a block on a side street right off Main.

Inside, there was a tree in the window and Christmas music playing. Animals and people of all ages filled the large reception area, which had a waiting room furnished with chairs and stationary animal toys—scratching posts, tubes for kids and dogs to scramble through. West thought it was pretty impressive for a shelter in such a small town.

A volunteer led them back to a large room full of kennels.

It was loud in there—dogs barking, kids laughing and talking over each other.

Alex glanced up at him and gave him a nervous little smile. "Okay. Let's do this." She slipped her hand in his. He liked how that felt, their fingers woven together, his warm palm pressed to her cool one, like they were a team, united against…

What?

He had no idea. Better to focus on the goal, which was to find her a short-haired male puppy of a medium to large breed.

They wandered from kennel to kennel. Many were already empty, the dogs who had stayed there having found themselves homes. She stopped at each one with an occupant. The dogs inside sniffed at her, most of them eager. Some ran in circles. Some nudged the bars and let out hopeful little whines.

She gave each dog her undivided attention for at least a minute or two—and then she moved on.

They had circled the room and were back near the door again when she glanced into the next kennel, eased her hand from his grip and dropped to a crouch.

At first, he thought the space was empty. But when he leaned in closer, he saw a small black-and-white dog with a pug nose and enormous black eyes sitting at the back wall of the kennel, staring straight ahead. That dog was no pup. It had salt-and-pepper hair around its nose and mouth. Even the white hair on its chest looked grayed.

Not a shorthair, either. Long, scraggly fur sprouted from the top of its head and made the floppy ears look longer still. "What is that, a shih tzu?" he asked.

Alex turned to him and put a finger to her lips. He shut his mouth, stuck his hands in his pockets and gave her a nod—hey, this was her moment. If she wanted him quiet, he wouldn't say a word.

She turned to the old dog at the back of the kennel. "Hello." The dog got up. Head high, the long fur of its curled tail bouncing, it trotted right to her, paws making click-clicking sounds on the concrete floor. Alex stuck a finger through the bars and scratched the mutt on its hairy head. "This is the one," she said.

The dog was the polar opposite of the dog she'd described in the car. It wasn't even male, from what he could see. "Right. A short-haired male puppy, medium to large. Just what you were looking for."

Alex shrugged. "Weston, I looked in those big eyes and I knew. She's the one." Turning back to the mutt, she asked, "You think you might want to come home with me?"

The dog reared up against the cage screen with an eager whine—a female, he could see that for certain now. Dropping back to all fours, she wagged her tangled tail, gave a tiny whine and then jumped three times in rapid succession. The jumping thing was damn cute. All four paws left the ground in unison. As she came down, her ears flew up. When she landed, the ears flopped down. At the same time, her claws clicked sharply on the concrete floor.

"She says yes," Alex informed him, as if she'd known the hairy little old lady dog all her life. She added, to the dog, "Okay, then. Let's get you out of there."

They learned as they filled out the paperwork that the old dog, a shih tzu mix as he'd suspected, had come to the shelter wearing a tag that read simply *Cookie*.

Alex shot him a triumphant glance, though he had no idea why until she explained, "'Cookie,' as in 'fortune.' See? When you know, you know."

The teenage volunteer behind the desk needed

a minute to process that, too. "Oh!" she said finally. "Like 'fortune cookie,' right?"

Alex nodded and flashed West a giant grin. "Cookie and me, we were meant to be."

Cookie thought so, too. She got up on her hind legs right there on the counter and swiped her long tongue all over Alex's face. Alex laughed, loving it. Whatever she'd decided earlier about the dog she would choose, Cookie was the one for her now.

"One thing," said the volunteer. "She never barks. Our vet says there's nothing wrong with her vocal cords. But still, she never barks."

Alex arched an eyebrow. "A quiet dog. I don't think that will be a problem for me."

The volunteer shrugged. "Just thought you should know."

Back at the cottage, after a detour to the pet store for supplies, Cookie settled right in. The dog followed Alex everywhere. As predicted by the girl behind the counter at the shelter, they had yet to hear a single bark. When spoken to, she aimed her black eyes right at you and stared as though soaking in your every word.

Alex spent a long time grooming the dog, talking to her softly, praising her as she brushed every tangle from her coat and trimmed her claws.

West could almost start to feel neglected. An

hour before they had to head to Halstead Farm for dinner, he managed to coax Alex back to bed for a quickie. Cookie followed them into the bedroom, but when Alex gave her a scratch on the head and said, "Go on now," the little dog turned around and trotted right back out the bedroom door, newly trimmed claws lightly tapping the floor.

"See?" Alex whipped her white sweater off over her head revealing a white satin bra he couldn't wait to get off her. "That dog is a treasure."

"Why are you still wearing so many clothes?" He was already stretched out on the bed naked. "I thought you said we had to be there at five thirty."

She gave him a slow look from under her lashes, her eyes pausing at his groin. "I like a man who's glad to see me."

And he was. Always. Very, very glad to see her—and not only in bed. He liked every damn thing about her, starting with her sharp mind and moving on to her great big heart.

She was the kind of woman he stayed away from as a rule. Dangerous to him, a threat to the freedom he'd always believed he needed. East was the steady one, the one who went to Stanford like their father while West rebelled and enrolled at UCLA. East had always wanted a family, same as their dad, a settled-down life with the right woman.

Not West. Yeah, someday he wanted kids. But he'd yet to fall in love. Losing his heart to a woman held zero appeal for him.

Or so he'd always believed…

Grabbing her hand, he pulled her down to the bed with him. She was laughing as he rolled her beneath him and bit the tip of her chin. "I might be jealous of that mutt," he said in a growl.

She eased her soft hands around his waist and stroked the skin at the small of his back. Impossibly, he grew harder. She whispered, "Let me kiss it all better."

He nibbled her earlobe. "Now you're talkin'."

West hated to leave the bed. But they were due at her sister's house for dinner. They had to get moving.

They got up. He put on his pants and she pulled on her robe. Her hair was all over the place and her cheeks were flushed pink. He couldn't resist grabbing her for one more long, deep kiss.

Before he was ready to let her go, she pulled back. "I need a quick shower."

Reluctantly, he released her. "Yeah, me, too."

"You first," she said. "Make it fast."

West emerged from the bathroom in ten minutes flat. Alex took her turn. By then, they were verging on late.

They put on their coats and Alex clipped Cookie's leash to her new collar. Off they went.

At Josie's, it was just the adults and baby David. Both of Miles's daughters were staying in town with their grandmother. Mostly, West had a good time. Miles was easy to talk to, though West didn't have a lot in common with the guy. They consoled each other about the Seahawks' so-so season and agreed it could be a good year for the Blazers.

As for Josie, Alex's middle sister made him a little nervous. More than once, West felt her eyes on him. He knew that look. It was a look his mother got whenever she thought anyone had dared even to think about doing wrong to one of her boys.

Message received. Loud and clear. If he broke her big sister's heart, Josie Halstead would very likely cut out his liver and have it for dinner.

He figured she would try to pull him aside somehow, to warn him that he'd better be good to Alex—or else. But she surprised him. Except for the occasional meaningful glance, she left him alone.

He was happy to get out of there when the evening was over.

"Let's take off for a couple of days," she said

at midnight. They were in her bed, naked, after more than one bout of energetic lovemaking.

He got up on an elbow to look down at her flushed face. “Right now?”

“Well, in the morning…”

He ran a finger across her clavicle, smoothed a stray lock of hair away from her cheek. “And go where?”

“How about Portland? We can stay at my place, get our Christmas shopping done.”

He kissed her, a quick one, though as soon as his lips met hers, he didn’t want to stop. It was kind of a problem. If he didn’t watch himself, he’d have her in a lip-lock constantly. “You know there’s the internet, right? You can get anything there and have it waiting on your doorstep within twenty-four hours.”

“But it’s Christmas. Half the fun is seeing the stores lit up, the Christmas music playing wherever you go, a wreath on every lamppost and a tree in all the windows.” She was frowning. “Right?”

He chuckled. “What? You’re not sure?”

“Well, I don’t do that myself. I don’t wander the stores, shopping for hours. It was always just work and more work and two days here at home if I’m lucky.”

He traced the shape of her softly parted lips, loving the pillowy texture while resisting the temptation to steal just one more kiss. Was he a goner? Maybe. And he would go anywhere with her—for her. Even Christmas shopping in actual brick-and-mortar stores.

And beyond his bizarre need to make sure she got her way in all things, he wouldn't mind staying at her place, spending a little time in her day-to-day world. "Okay, then. We'll go to Portland tomorrow."

She scoffed. "Wait. What? Yes? Just like that?"

"Just like that. It's settled. Now, kiss me."

She tipped up that sweet mouth and he claimed it. They didn't get to sleep until after two.

Chapter Nine

"I don't know..." Alex had her key in one hand and Cookie's leash in the other. They stood at the door to Alex's apartment in a modern building on Northwest Lovejoy Street. The little dog gazed up at Alex intently.

West let a few seconds elapse before asking, "What's wrong?"

Alex slid him a doubtful glance. And then she drew herself up. "Nothing. Really. Let's go in."

West knew as well as the dog did that something was bothering her. Her doorstep was not the right place to get into it, though. "Good idea."

She stuck the key in the lock and pushed the door open to a long hallway with doors branching off to either side. They hung their coats in the closet right there by the door and then she led him into the master suite. It was nice in a generic way, with the en suite near the hall door. The bedroom itself had a good-sized window that looked out on Northwest Ninth.

Alex bent to unclip Cookie's leash. Tags clinking, the little dog shook herself, and then headed back out the bedroom door. He could hear her claws tapping hardwood as she bustled off down the hallway.

"Just leave the bags here," Alex said. He wheeled them under the window and collapsed the handles.

"Great." Her smile was too wide. "Come on. I'll show you around."

They proceeded down the long hallway. She pointed out the other bathroom on the left and the smaller bedroom she used as a home office at the end.

The living room was the eyepopper, with windows that curved around the facade of the building, giving gorgeous views of Lovejoy and Ninth Avenue. "Nice," he said.

She bent and scooped up her dog. "I took it after Rob and I broke up."

"The homebody from Utah."

"Right. It's a lease. I wasn't ready to buy at that point. I saw the view—the pretty bakery across the street, the streetcar going by. It lifted my spirits."

"I get that."

She set the dog back down and approached a wilted potted plant in the window. "Poor thing. I think it's done for."

He grabbed her hand, reeled her in and wrapped his arms around her. She gazed up at him with a determined little smile.

His heart ached at the lost look on her face. Not sure what to say, he kissed her instead. When he lifted his head, he encircled her throat with his hand, tipping her face up to him, so she wouldn't look away. "Tell me the truth. Do you want to sleep here tonight?"

It took her several seconds to come out with it. "No, I don't. It's a great apartment, but it reminds me of the past, of the life I won't be living anymore—and a little bit of all the things I still haven't figured out yet."

He cradled the side of her beautiful face. "Back to Heartwood, then?"

That brought a grin. "You're much too agreeable. I just dragged us to Portland and you're ready to turn right around and head home to Wild Rose."

He kissed the space between her eyebrows. "There. Here. Doesn't matter to me. I like being with you. We'll be doing that either way."

She hummed low in her throat and he thought about sliding his hands over her fine ass and downward to the back of her thighs. Then he would lift her as he guided her legs to wrap around his waist… "But I do want this little Christmas trip," she said. "I want the holiday shopping. I want to spend a few days here in Portland, just you and me. I also *don't* want to explain to Josie why I told her this morning that we were heading to Portland for a few days—and then three hours later, there we are back at the farm. I love her. I love her kids. I think Miles is a wonderful man, that he's *almost* good enough for my sister. But I do not need another pity dinner at Halstead Farm."

"One, I don't think they're pity dinners."

"Yeah, well. You're not the one being pitied."

"Two, can't you just tell Josie we're fine on our own for dinner?"

"Of course I can," she grumbled. "But I still want a few days away from the farm."

"Then let's go."

"Go where? What about Cookie? We'll need to stay somewhere that takes pets."

"No problem. I know the place."

He got them a suite at the Cascadia, a pet-friendly Wright property just south of the Pearl District, near Pioneer Courthouse Square. The hotel had a list of highly rated dog sitters, so that Cookie had someone to look after her when they went shopping or out to eat.

That afternoon, he drove Alex to Washington Square Mall, where she led him around from shop to shop. He mostly did what men tend to do in shopping malls, waiting around while she bought stuff and then carrying her bags and packages.

It wasn't anything he hadn't done before. He'd had a lot of girlfriends over the years and the majority of them liked to shop. The difference for him was that he didn't mind it one damn bit when it was Alex he was following around as she tried to decide what to get for the twins and whether her aunt Marilyn might want one of those giant KitchenAid mixers in a primary color, the kind of appliance that did everything but your laundry.

They got back to the hotel at a little after five, sent the dog sitter on her way and decided on room service for dinner. Again, they were up half the night doing all his favorite things—the ones you do while naked.

Yeah. A shopping trip with Alex? Count him in.

Monday, they shopped until early afternoon. It was a gorgeous almost-winter day, the sky a flawless blue with very little wind. They let the dog sitter go and took Cookie for a walk down Broadway to Market and over to PSU Park. He'd found a backpack pet carrier that day, though Alex had sworn she couldn't see Cookie putting up with being strapped in the thing.

West bought it anyway. He could always take it back if the dog refused to get in it. But after the twenty-minute walk to the park and another half hour of wandering around the Portland State University campus, Cookie seemed perfectly happy to let Alex slip her into the pack on West's back. That night, they ate at the rooftop restaurant right there at the Cascadia.

They were enjoying their beef tenderloin skewers and chili-glazed noodles with sweet peppers and mushrooms when someone behind him said, "Alex? How are you?"

Alex put on a polite smile. "Jerome, good to see you…"

A slim, well-dressed balding man emerged from behind West to stand beside their table. Alex introduced them. Jerome was a former client of hers.

"I heard you left KJ&T," he said. "I can't believe they let you go. Where are you now? Same cell number?"

"I'm taking a little time off," she replied, not answering either of his questions. She looked so relaxed, in command. Unruffled. If West hadn't known she'd quit because her fortune cookie told her to, he would assume she'd given the usual notice and had moved on to something better at a firm even bigger than the one she'd left behind.

"Well, we need to stay in touch," said Jerome.

"It's so good to see you, Jerome."

The older man gave a low laugh. "Definitely. A pleasure."

She nodded, dismissing him. "Take care." She waited until he was well out of earshot to say, "It's so strange. I've lived in Portland for almost a decade. I know a lot of people here in town, but somehow they're all either business colleagues, clients and former clients, or casual acquaintances. Shouldn't I have made at least one true friend?"

He reached across the table and took her hand. "You worked long hours and your hometown is nearby. It's not surprising that you wanted to go back to Heartwood when you finally got a day or two off."

She stared down at their joined hands. "But a girlfriend or two, you know? Someone to hang with, go to happy hour with. I should have made a good friend or two..." Her gaze shifted upward to meet his. She stared at him through troubled eyes.

And she was clutching his hand pretty hard

now. Strangely, he didn't mind that at all. On the contrary, he wished she would never let go.

And that wasn't like him. Not like him in the least.

The last thing he'd ever wanted was someone to hold on tight. He liked to keep it easy. Light. Fun. Finding the "right" woman to settle down with sounded like something he was bound to do badly. His father had that. East had always wanted that—and East had it now, with Payton. East and Myron Wright were happy men, steady men who knew what they wanted and went after it.

West envied them their happiness at the same time as he didn't understand them in the least. He had a certain restlessness inside him. He didn't want to be like his dad or his brother. He was his own man. He went into every new relationship knowing it wouldn't last, scoping out the exits so he could bow out with no fuss when the woman realized he wasn't relationship material—or worse, started wanting more than he had in him to give.

But Alex…

When she clung to him for comfort, he just wished she'd cling harder. He didn't get it.

But so what? They had a month to be together and so far, he was loving every minute of it.

"There's something wrong with me," she said.

"There is nothing wrong with you."

Her thumb brushed slowly across the back of his hand, stirring the nerve endings, rousing him up. Her eyes had gone from anxious to something much softer, something willing. Something very, very hot. "I give up," she said in a husky little whisper. "You win. There is nothing wrong with me."

"That's the spirit."

"Weston. Your eyes just got darker. What *are* you thinking?"

"Guess."

"Hmm. We should go back to the suite."

"Look at you, counselor. Nailed it on the first try."

In the suite, Alex cuddled Cookie as West tipped the dog sitter and showed her out.

When he shut the door, he engaged the security lock and turned those eyes of his on her. They were so dark now, his eyes, like midnight—midnight and all the secret, naughty things people do when the lights are out. "It is just possible that you are the sexiest man I've ever known."

He gave her a long, considering sort of look, like he was trying to decide what exactly he wanted to do with her. Finally, he instructed, "Put Cookie in her bed and tell her to stay there."

Alex buried her nose in the soft ruff around

Cookie's neck. "Cookie doesn't like to be ordered around."

"Then ask her nicely. Do. It. Now."

"It's so hot when you say my fortune to me."

"Do I need to say it again?"

"Oh, yes. Please."

"Do it now, Alex."

She took her time, setting Cookie in the doggy bed, petting her some more, giving her little loving scratches and calling her smart and such a good dog. Finally, with a long huff of breath, Cookie put her head on her little graying paws and shut her black eyes.

By then, West was leaning in the doorway to the bedroom, broad chest and feet bare. Alex rose and went to him. "Thank you."

"For...?"

"Being with me now, making everything easy and fun when I don't have a clue what I'm doing. Not asking questions, just...bringing me here to this nice hotel when I couldn't bear to stay in my own apartment."

"You're doing fine, Alex."

Was she? "Not so sure about that. But you are definitely making everything better."

He eased his hand up under her hair to cradle the back of her head. "I have a question."

"Ask me anything."

"Why do you still have so many clothes on?"

Moving in closer, right up against him, she nuzzled him under that sculpted jaw of his. "You should take them off me." She smiled against his skin as he unzipped her snug wool dress.

"I have done all my Christmas shopping and then some," Alex announced Wednesday afternoon as they left Powell's City of Books, each of them lugging a giant bag full of books, games and intriguing stationery supplies she thought her sisters might appreciate.

It was raining. West took her free hand and smiled at the way she twined her fingers with his. They ran to the corner and ducked into the parking garage. Once they were under the concrete shelter of the stairwell, she grabbed the collar of his coat and leaned in close. "Can I tell you a secret?" she whispered.

She could tell him any damn thing she pleased. Whatever she wanted, he just wanted to make it happen for her. "Hit me with it."

"I don't want to go back to Wild Rose yet."

He kissed her, because kissing her was one of his favorite things and her mouth was right there, tipped up to him, tempting him. Her lips were cool and wet from the rain. When she pulled back, he asked, “So if we’re not going back to Heartwood, what *are* we doing?”

“Good question…”

They started down the stairs to the car.

“Maybe we could just stay at the hotel forever,” she said wistfully as they loaded the bags in back.

He grabbed her arm, pulled her close and kissed her once more. “I don’t see that as a long-term plan.”

“Eh. Maybe not.”

Halfway back to the hotel, her phone chimed with a text. She pulled it from the pocket of her coat and read it. “It’s Josie. She wants to know how I’m doing…”

He glanced at her. She stared out the windshield, frowning. Did she need a nudge? Probably. “Tell your sister you miss her and we’ll be back at Wild Rose tonight.”

“Look at you. All decisive and forceful.”

“I get it. You don’t like it when I tell you what to do.”

“Cookie doesn’t like it. As for me, au contraire. I find it extraordinarily sexy. And hot—did I ever mention that I find you hot?”

“You might have, once or twice.”

“I’m a mess, huh?” She blew out her cheeks with a hard breath. “Never mind. Don’t answer that. I'm texting her right now, letting her know that we'll be back at the farm tonight."

They arrived at Wild Rose that night at eight. Together, they slogged back and forth in a foot of new snow, carrying the shopping bags, luggage, Cookie and all her stuff inside.

"I should go see my sister," Alex said once they'd finished unloading the car.

He kissed her and handed her his key. "Take the Range Rover. It's right out in front."

At Josie's, Davy was in bed, the girls were upstairs, and Miles gave Alex a hug before disappearing into the office at the back of the house.

Josie made tea and they sat at the kitchen counter. "Thanks for coming over." She reached out and clasped Alex's shoulder. "How was Portland?"

"Good. Really good..."

"Then why do you have that doubtful look on your face?"

Who could she tell the truth to if not her sister? "We were going to stay at my place."

"But you didn't?"

"West ended up getting us a suite at the Cascadia downtown because I walked in the door of my apartment and I just wanted out. I don't want to live there anymore."

"Ah, Ax..." Josie was a great hugger. She pulled Alex close and gave her a good, long squeeze, then took her by the arms and stared straight in her eyes. "Then don't."

Alex totally agreed. "After the holidays, I'm clearing the place out and giving my notice that I won't be renewing when my lease is up in February."

"So you'll stay here in Heartwood for a while, then?"

"I have no idea. But I won't be in that apartment. Wherever I end up, I want to buy a house, I think. It's time I had my own home. I can certainly afford one."

"Yes, you can." Josie sipped her tea. "I am dying to ask how things are with Weston."

"Terrific. He's a great guy on every level and I love hanging out with him." Alex put on her stern face. "But do not get stars in your eyes, Josephine. It's just for the holidays with West and me."

Josie put up both hands. "All right, all right. I get it. And I'm glad the two of you are having a good time. How's Cookie?"

"I think I'm in love. She's the best. West bought her a backpack. We walked to PSU twice and when she got tired, West carried her around on his back. She was so cute—I have pictures." She whipped out her phone and showed off several shots of Cookie in the backpack with her tongue hanging out.

"Adorable." Josie gave Alex a sweet little smile. "West looks smitten." He'd glanced over his shoulder at her as she snapped the picture.

"Yeah, he likes Cookie almost as much as I do."

"Alex. Cookie's a sweetheart. But that man is not looking at Cookie."

"Stop. I mean it. We're having fun." She held the phone closer to her sister's face. "*He's* having fun and that's why he's smiling in this shot."

"Whatever you say..."

"Josie, you really are a hopeless romantic. You realize that, don't you?"

"No, I'm not. I'm a realist, through and through."

"Yeah, right."

"Give me a little credit. You *are* talking to the woman who gave up on men completely, the woman who had IUI to get her beautiful baby boy because she actually believed she was through with men. And look at me now, completely in love with Miles. There's a lesson in that, Alex. Because nobody is through with love. They just aren't, no matter what they say."

"And I did not say I was through with love. I'm only saying, not now. No way. I've got... issues, stuff I have to figure out before I'll be ready to consider getting anything serious going with a man."

Josie pursed up her soft mouth like she'd just sucked something sour. "Love does not wait for a convenient time. Love sneaks up on you when you least expect it."

"So love's like a stalker? Is that what you're telling me?"

"Your cynicism is disturbing—more tea?"

"Only if you promise to stop lecturing me about love."

Josie poured her another cup. They moved on to less fraught subjects, things like further improvements Alex wanted to make at Wild Rose and the Christmas gifts she'd bought for Hazel and Ashley during her Portland shopping spree.

When she got back to the cottage, West and Cookie were snoozing on the sofa in the glow of the Christmas tree lights while *The Shawshank Redemption* played on the flat-screen over the fireplace—with subtitles and the sound down low.

Alex dropped West's car key in the bowl by the door, hung up her jacket and took off her boots. Cookie jumped down and bustled over to greet her, then headed for the kitchen.

"Get over here." West tapped the empty space the dog had left behind. Alex snuggled up on the sofa with him, tucking herself in against him, spoon-fashion.

He ran a hand down the outside of her arm and along her outer thigh to her knee. Beneath the sleeve of her turtleneck, her skin prickled with pleasure at his touch. "I have to go to Seattle tomorrow early," he said against her ear. "Be back Friday, late afternoon."

She let out a sad little whine to let him know she would miss him.

He kissed the side of her head. "Meetings. You won't even know I'm gone."

She took his hand and threaded her fingers between his.

They watched the rest of the movie without either of them saying a word.

Alex woke the next morning alone in her bed. "West?" Faintly, she could hear the shower running.

When she tapped on the bathroom door, he called out, "It's open!"

She stuck her head in and thought as she often did that no man should be allowed to look that good naked. They grinned at each other through the water-beaded glass of the shower door. She asked, "Want coffee before you go?"

"Nah. Gotta get moving."

"I'll fill you a travel mug..."

"Perfect."

Twenty minutes later, she stood by the tree in the front window, watching his Range Rover drive away.

West got to the office at eleven. He spent an hour with the planning team and then went to lunch with the accountants. Back at the office, he had another meeting in one of the conference rooms. It lasted until four.

He was just settling in behind his desk again when Easton appeared at his door. “Let’s get a drink, you and me.” When West hesitated, anticipating more crap about his Christmas fling with Alex, East said, “Not going to ambush you. Truth is, I miss your face when you’re not around.”

They went to Oliver’s. East really did seem to have no agenda. He talked about his boys playing angels in the Christmas show at school. They both chuckled at that. Penn and Bailey were great kids—but they were no more angels than Weston and East had been at that age.

The boys would be on their Christmas break starting a week from Saturday. The Wright family contingent, including the grandparents, would be caravanning down to Wild Rose as usual.

“Enjoy the peace and quiet while it lasts,” East advised.

West smiled and thought about Alex. What

was she doing right now? He wanted to call her, listen to her tell him every last detail of her day so far, even though he'd left her just that morning and he would have her in his arms again tomorrow night.

"West?"

"Hmm?"

"Still with me?"

"Yeah. Just thinking…"

"About Alex?"

Why lie? "Yeah. I really like her, East. *More* than like her." He barked out a laugh at the stunned look on East's face. "What's the matter? What'd I do now?"

East drew a slow breath. "You sound serious, that's all. And you are never serious about a woman—maybe Naomi. But with Naomi, it was more that you were *trying* to be serious about her, because of the baby…"

West held up two fingers. Their server nodded and headed for the bar. "I *am* serious about Alex."

East took several seconds to digest that bit of information. Finally he replied, "That's certainly a first."

"Exactly. I always thought it was me, you know? That I just wasn't like you and dad, wasn't built for the whole get-married-and-make-babies life. But now I'm starting to see it was only that

I hadn't met the right person yet—and please. I know you and Payton tell each other everything, but…"

East finished his drink. "I'm making an exception in this case. Under certain circumstances, a man should have a right to talk to his brother without anyone else having to know what gets said—not even his brother's wife."

"Thank you."

The server appeared with another round. West waited until she left to say, "You know Alex is making changes, maybe deciding on a different direction career-wise?"

"Yeah."

"She's starting over. We spent some time together in Portland this week. She doesn't seem at all invested in living there. I'm thinking of suggesting that she might move here to Seattle. She'd have a bigger job market. You guys are here, so she'll have family close by. It's not *that* far from Wild Rose. And from the way she talked while we were in Portland, it seemed to me that she might be ready for a new town, a fresh start."

East cut right through all the bull. "You want her close."

Why equivocate? "Yeah. I want more time with her. I want to see where this goes with us—I mean, I already know where *I* want it to go, but

I'm thinking I would have a better chance to make it last with her if she were here, in town."

East was nodding. "Makes sense to me."

"We have an agreement, though. It's just until New Year's. Then we go our separate ways. Alex has given no indication she might be willing to keep seeing me after the holidays."

Across the table, East chuckled. "I had an agreement with Payton once upon a time."

"I remember. Just for a week, wasn't it?"

"That damn agreement screwed up my life—and hers *and* the boys'—for years. I think you should learn from my mistake."

"You're right. I get it."

East grinned. "But look on the bright side. Even if Alex refuses to change the plan, you're still in better shape for working it out than I was. No matter where she runs off to, she's not leaving the family and neither are you. You'll always have a way to stay in touch. You'll see her at holidays and family occasions."

"If we're not together, that's going to be grim."

"Yes, it will—and truthfully, West. What were you guys thinking?"

"That we wanted each other. That neither of us wanted a real relationship. That we could both walk away when January rolled around." *After all, we walked away once before.*

East leaned in. "I know that look, Weston.

Whatever it is, just put it out there. You need to talk to someone. We both know that—and I meant what I said. I won't tell Payton if you don't want me to."

West did need the feedback. He also had a feeling that Alex would be okay with him telling East about that first night. "The night you and Payton got married…?"

"Yeah?"

"Alex and I spent it together out at the house on the river."

East caught on immediately. "That was the night you learned that Leo had died."

"That's right. I got the call from Leo's mom and I left the wedding reception. I started thinking I was going to be sick. Halfway to the river house, I had to pull over. I was standing on the side of the road waiting for your wedding cake to make a reappearance when Alex pulled in behind me. She drove me to the river house. She made that night bearable. We agreed it was just that one time and nobody in the families ever had to know—and yeah, I get the irony. That was our first agreement and we didn't keep it."

East said nothing. He knew when to wait, knew to let a man get it all out.

West confessed, "I've been lying to myself through most of this year. I tried not to think of her and I told myself repeatedly that she rarely crossed my mind."

"So then. Time to revise the current agreement?"

"I think we both know the answer to that."

Chapter Ten

Alex had kept busy all that day. She wrapped half of the endless array of presents she'd bought in Portland.

As afternoon rolled around, she reminded herself that she really ought to brush up her résumé, call a couple of headhunters she knew…

But that was the problem. She had no idea what she was looking for. She didn't know what she wanted to do with the rest of her life. How could she start looking for a new job when she still hadn't decided what kind of job she wanted?

So instead of focusing on what her next career move ought to be, she vacuumed and dusted. That night, she watched rom-coms back-to-back.

It was wonderful. Alone time. Every woman needed it. She didn't miss her Christmas lover. How silly would that be? It was a casual, just-for-now thing they had together anyway.

The next day she wrapped the rest of the presents and made stew.

And when West drove up at four thirty, her silly heart did gymnastics inside her chest. She and Cookie ran out to greet him. As soon as she got him inside, they were kissing wildly, tearing at each other's clothes as they fell across her bed.

Much later, they got up, ate some of the stew she'd had in the slow cooker all day and then went right back to bed. She must have dropped off to sleep at some point.

When she woke, he was up on an elbow, staring down at her.

"What? Do I have stew on my chin?"

He bent close and licked her there. "Nope. You're good—and very tasty."

She hooked an arm around his neck and brought his mouth right down to an inch from hers. "You were looking extremely serious for a minute there. Come on now. No thoughtful frowns. It's Christmastime in our own sweet little Christmas cottage. Let's be jolly."

He brushed a kiss across her lips, propped his head on his hand and stared at her some more.

"West. You're doing it again."

"I like looking at you."

She pulled him down for another quick kiss. "While you were gone, I was thinking that we should do things..."

"Things like...?"

"Things you do on vacation at Christmas. Do you ski?"

"I do."

"I don't, not really. I've never had the time for leisure pursuits. But I have the time now and I'm not letting inexperience stop me."

His eyes were the brightest blue right then, like sapphires. "I didn't bring my skis."

"Live dangerously," she challenged. "Rent them."

The next day, they dropped Cookie off at Josie's and went skiing at Mount Hood Meadows—well, West went skiing. Alex fooled around on the beginner slopes and then had a drink at one of the bars.

Tuesday, they got lucky and managed to book a room up at Timberline Lodge. Josie and her stepdaughters had fallen in love with Cookie and offered to dog sit anytime. So they left the dog at Josie's and had a three-night getaway in the knotty pine splendor of the famous old hotel built in 1937. They slept late every morning and made love in the afternoons.

Time didn't exist and yet it passed much too quickly.

All of a sudden, it was the Saturday before Christmas Eve and the family arrived. Everyone showed up that day—Auntie M and Ernesto, Joyce and Myron, Payton, Easton and the twins, too. They all went to Josie's for a big chicken dinner and then played charades until after ten.

Alex kept expecting someone to remark on West's unplanned two-week stay in the guest cottage, but no one said a word—except Joyce, who only mentioned how great she thought it was that West had taken some time off over the holidays.

Back at the cottage, Alex took West straight to bed. They didn't get to sleep until well past midnight. She dropped off thinking how good it felt to have his arms around her. Their Christmas fling was half-over. Time was racing by far too fast.

Too soon, he would head back to Seattle to stay. It made her sad to think of sleeping without him.

But she knew she was just being self-indulgent. Neither of them wanted anything permanent. She didn't even know where she would be living come January. Not her apartment, no way. She really did not want to go back there. Like her years at KJ&T, the apartment seemed a testimony to a life chosen long ago, a life of working her ass off to make lots of money as a cushion against some unknown future disaster. A life that had turned out to be not only unnecessary, but empty, somehow.

Uh-uh. She wouldn't be going back to her old place except to clean it out.

As for her and West, they had two weeks more together and that would have to be enough—scratch that. It *would* be enough. The goal right now was to savor every second. She dropped off to sleep with a smile on her face—and woke sometime later.

It was still dark. She had the strangest, loneliest feeling and slid her hand across the bottom sheet seeking the warmth of the man beside her.

He wasn't there.

She sat up. Flickering light bled in under her shut bedroom door and Cookie's bed was empty.

With a yawn, she put on her fuzzy slippers and her giant sleep cardigan, raked her fingers through the wild nest of her hair and went to find out where West had gone.

She didn't have to look far. He was stretched out on the couch under the fleecy Christmas blanket printed with snowflakes and reindeer that she'd found on their Portland shopping trip. Cookie had curled herself up in a ball beside him. An old Eddie Murphy movie played quietly on the flat-screen.

"Hey," he said, as her dog jumped down and came right to her.

"Hey." She scooped up the sweet mutt and buried her face in the fountain of graying black fur sprouting from the top of Cookie's head. "I woke up. You weren't there..." She couldn't quite read his expression. A little bit watchful, maybe.

His eyes seemed full of questions. "Been thinking." He pushed the blanket away, sat up and held out his hand.

She had the strangest sensation right then, like someone had dribbled ice water down her spine. "Everything okay?"

"Everything is wonderful. Come here. Sit with me."

She set Cookie on the floor and went to him. Laying her hand in his, she let him pull her down to sit beside him.

He turned off the movie, leaving them bathed in the glow of the Christmas tree lights—until he switched on the lamp at the end of the sofa.

Something was wrong, she just knew it. "Are you leaving? Is that it?" She felt heartbroken that he might go—and how ridiculous was that? They were just having fun. It was only till New Year's anyway.

"No," he said, facing her, easing his hand under her hair and wrapping his fingers around the back of her neck. His palm felt so warm and strong.

She found such comfort in his touch and wished he would never let go, then quickly reminded herself not to do that. Of course he would let go. They would both let go, as agreed, when the time came.

He pulled her closer. His warm breath brushed her cheek. “Leaving is the last thing I want to do.” Relief, like cool water on a fevered wound, poured through her.

And then he kissed her, a slow kiss.

“Whew,” she said when their eyes met once more. “Had me scared there for a minute.”

He kissed her again, quick and hard this time. “Alex, I’ve never done this before and I have no idea *how* to do it.”

She scanned his face, searching for clues, for the source of this strange mood of his. “Done what?”

He shut his eyes and added prayerfully, “God help me not to screw this up.”

Her heart started beating too fast all over again. “West. What is it? Tell me.”

“I’m just going to go ahead and say it.” Now he looked desperate, as though he stood on the edge of some emotional cliff and debated the wisdom of jumping off.

She captured his face between her hands and pleaded, “Listen, whatever it is, it can’t be that bad, it really can't. You need to just say it, put it out there. And we'll deal with it."

He actually chuckled. "I didn't say it was bad."

She let her hands stray down to rest on his wide shoulders and gave them a squeeze. "It isn't?" When he slowly shook his head, she dropped her hands to her lap and confessed, "I have no idea what is going on here. I'm completely in the dark. Please. Whatever it is, just tell me."

"Come here." He gathered her close. It felt so good, his arms around her. She buried her face in the warm crook of his neck. He said, soft and low, "I'm in love with you, Alex."

It was absolutely the last thing she'd ever expected to hear coming out of his mouth. She jerked her head back and blinked up at him, stunned. "Wait. What?"

"Yes." He took both her hands. She resisted the urge to yank them away, to jump all over him for saying such a completely unhinged, impossible thing. And then he went and said it again. "I love you. You're the one for me."

"But I… I mean, you…" She had no clue what to say and not the faintest idea how to feel.

This was not a good time to start talking about love. Her life was a mess. *She* was a mess. She had money running out her ears and what good did all that money do her, when she'd come unmoored? She had no idea what to do with the rest of her life. Didn't he realize what a bad bet she was?

Apparently not. He was still sitting there holding her hands, patiently waiting for her to speak.

Easing her fingers free of his grip, she pushed some words out. "I mean, seriously? You have to know that I'm not a good risk. Right now, all I have going for me is money. And I know you already have plenty of that."

His eyes held only tenderness. "I'll take that risk. In a heartbeat. And believe me, I knew this would freak you out. I knew I should just keep my mouth shut—but, Alex, I need you to know. I need you to start letting yourself imagine how it might be, the two of us, together for more than just Christmas."

"The two of us," she parroted. Because she still could not get her mind around what he'd just said to her. "But it's a fling. We agreed. It *is* just for now."

"How many ways can I say it? I'm very clear on our agreement and just for now isn't cutting it for me anymore. Alex, I'm only asking you to think about it. As a possibility. Please say you'll consider the idea of you and me staying together after New Year's."

"But I just said I can't do that. I'm not ready for that."

"And that's why I'm telling you exactly how I

feel. I want you. I love you. You're the woman I never expected to find. You're brave and strong and ready to take on the world."

"No. No, I'm not any of those things right now."

"Yes, you are. Alex, you're a hero. You'll do whatever you have to do to make sure your sisters and your aunt have what they need. You're beautiful. Every time I look at you I want to get you naked. I think you're amazing. You're like nobody else I've ever known. You're the one, Alexandra. The one for me, the one I honestly believed didn't even exist. And I love you. I do. I just need you to ask yourself if I could be the one for you."

"But I..." Words. She simply didn't have them. When she opened her mouth, everything she'd already said came out all over again. "West, it's just for Christmas, remember? Just for now. That's what we agreed."

He was onto her. "You're repeating yourself."

"I know," she replied wretchedly. "Because I don't even know what to say right now."

"That's all right. You don't *have* to say anything more right now. Just think about it, won't you? Just consider the idea of making a new agreement with me."

"A new agreement..." She shook her head. "I can't. I'm not ready for anything like that."

His eyes were kind. Gentle. Patient. "You didn't want to stay in your own apartment. I got the feeling you weren't even sure that you wanted to live in Portland anymore."

"You're right. I'm not keeping the apartment. And I'm not sure where I'll be living. What's that got to do with anything?"

"Do you still want to live in Portland?"

She didn't, not really, but if she said that, it would only look like more of a reason to give Seattle a chance. "I'm not sure yet."

"Well, I'm sure. I want to be with you. I want us to stay together after the holidays are over. And Seattle would be a good choice for you. It's a bigger town. You'd have a wider range of possibilities for whatever you decide to do next. Move in with me if you're ready for that. Or get your own place. Wake up every morning in bed with me. Or see me once a week—to start. We can take it as slow and careful as you need it to be. What do you say?"

Nothing. She had nothing.

He tried again. "However you want it, Alex, we can work it all out. Even if you're not sure about Seattle, I'm willing to try long-distance. We can see how that goes. Just think about giving us a chance to be more than a fling. Just consider not walking away when January comes around."

She wanted to say yes. So much. But wouldn't that just be taking advantage of his feelings for her, getting lost in their love affair to keep from figuring out what to do with the rest of her life? She could wake up one morning and realize she'd only been using him.

He didn't need that. He deserved so much more from the woman he loved.

"I can't do that, West. I don't even know where I'm going yet. I can't just move to Seattle and be with you. And the long-distance thing, well, the problem would still be there. I can't even imagine trying to maintain a relationship right now. I have no idea yet what I want to do next."

"I get that. It's a problem that you have to solve for yourself. All I'm asking is why not do it in Seattle? And if not in Seattle, then at least let's stay together, be a long-distance couple. Let's see each other whenever we can."

"I'm just no good at the love thing, West. I'm really not. I have trouble trusting men."

He slapped a hand against his heart like he was kidding around. But the real pain in his eyes told another story. "That hurts. Now I'm 'men'? You're putting me in the same category as your cheating ex-husband and the weird guy from Utah?"

"No! That's not what I meant, it's really not..."

His eyes had turned sad. "Will you give it some thought?"

"West..." She reached out.

He moved back, clear of her touch. "Will you think about it, Alex? Yes or no."

She longed to say yes, that she would definitely consider his offer, that she didn't want to lose him after New Year's, that she would love to keep seeing him, to move to his town and make a life with him there. But clinging to him right now wouldn't be right.

"Was that a no?" he asked too quietly.

"West, first and foremost, I need to figure out my life on my own. I can't afford to be distracted by a new relationship at this point."

"Got it. I'm 'men' and I'm a distraction."

"No, that's not what I said..."

"It's exactly what you said."

This was all going sideways and she didn't know how to stop the slide. She searched for the words that would slow this disaster down. "I'm wild about you. But fun and togetherness for the holidays is one thing and—"

"Stop." When she fell silent, he continued, "Let me tell you where you just said we are with this. After the holidays, you and I are through. You are not moving to Seattle. You won't try long-distance, won't try being with me whenever you can. You refuse to give either issue any more thought because you will never change your mind. Is that right?"

Her heart ached so bad and her mind reeled. Somehow, she made herself breathe slow and even. She could not take him up on his offer and she needed to own that. No drama, no whining. No more repeating the same excuses over and over.

"Yes, West. That's right."

"Fair enough, then." He stood. "I'm going to bed."

She had to steel herself not to beg him, *Don't go. Come on, West. We can work it out...*

What was there to work out? He wanted what she wasn't willing to give. She'd hurt him and he couldn't bear to be around her right now. The least she could do for him was to just let him go.

He disappeared through the arch into the hallway. A moment later she heard the door to the back bedroom click shut.

Cookie whined. Alex glanced over and saw that the old lady dog was sitting at the end of the coffee table, giant black eyes full of sympathy and unconditional love.

"I'll just leave him alone for now," Alex whispered. "We'll talk some more in the morning. I'll smooth things over. It will be all right."

Cookie just stared at her, the wisdom of the ages in those big, sad eyes.

"I guess we should go to bed, too, huh?"

Cookie didn't answer.

Alex rose, picked up the dog and returned to her room, hesitating at the threshold as she debated the pros and cons of shutting her door.

In the end, she left it open and took Cookie in bed with her.

Around three, she got up again to let Cookie out for a minute. West's door was still shut.

When she brought the dog back in, she shut her own door. And then she felt foolish. Who did she think she was kidding? If he came to her, she would let him in. Why pretend otherwise?

She opened the door and got back in bed. Little good that did. She hardly slept at all.

At six in the morning, she heard his door open. He went into the bathroom. She heard the shower running. A few minutes after the shower stopped, he returned to his room.

Coffee, she decided. She'd had enough of lying there wide-awake, ears straining to catch the slightest hint of movement from the back bedroom.

When he spoke, she was standing at the sink, sipping her first cup of coffee, staring out the window as the sky slowly lightened toward dawn.

"Alex."

Her heart rate spiked. She drew a slow, calming breath before she turned. He was standing on the far side of the island fully dressed. Across the great room, she spotted his big roller suitcase. He'd left it at the front door with a smaller bag beside it.

"Coffee?" she asked. His face was set against her, but she tried anyway. "I was hoping we could talk."

"You've got something new to say?"

She set down her mug very carefully in order not to bang it against the counter so hard that it shattered. "No, I really don't. But it's not fair of you to just get up and go. We had an agreement and now you want to change it. And because I don't, you're moving to the Heartwood Inn or whatever?"

"It's not about what's fair, Alex. And no, I'm not going to the Heartwood Inn. I'm going back to Seattle."

Now she wanted to throw the damn mug at him. "But it's Christmas. The family will—"

"They'll get over it. I don't want to be here. I'm not in a holiday mood right now. I'll stop by Payton's cottage and let them know I'm leaving."

She almost started shrieking at him. But come on. Facts were facts. He wanted more. She didn't. Even if he had some coffee and they talked, the outcome would in all likelihood remain the same. They stood on opposite sides of a great divide.

"Hey," he said gently.

She realized she was staring into her coffee mug, lost in her own misery. Lifting her head, she met his eyes. "Okay, West. I get it. I don't *want* to get it, but I do. I've got no right to give you a hard time about leaving."

"Then stop."

"Yes. All right." She tried her best to put on a wobbly smile. "I want you to know that these past couple of weeks with you have been so good. The best ever, truly."

"Yeah." His fine mouth twitched at the corner, but he failed to return her smile. "Too bad about the way it's ending. I'm new at this love thing. I guess I've made a mess of it."

"No. You put it right out there. Even though I'm not saying yes, I admire that so much. You're braver than I am."

He gave her a slow nod. "Yes, I am."

Cookie stood at his feet staring up at him expectantly.

He gathered her into his arms, buried his face in her ruff and then scratched her head. "You take care of Alex, now." Cookie licked his cheek. He dipped to a crouch and set her back down. "I'll miss you, Alex."

"And I'll miss you." So damn much. It was going to be bad. Really bad.

"See you," he said. "Probably from across the table at some future family dinner."

She locked her knees to keep from darting around the island, grabbing his arm and begging him to stay. “Bye, West.”

A minute later, the front door closed behind him.

Chapter Eleven

Alex stood by the tree and watched out the window until West emerged from Payton's cottage, climbed into his Range Rover and drove away.

Ten minutes later, Payton came out, ran down the steps and along the driveway to the guest cottage.

Alex opened the door as her sister came up the steps. The minute Payton was inside, she grabbed Alex in a hug. They stood with their arms around each other, holding on tight, Payton's giant belly cradled between them, rocking each other from side to side.

"Josie and Auntie M will be right over," Payton whispered in her ear.

Alex was the one who pulled back. She took Payton by the shoulders. "Coffee?"

"I shouldn't." She stroked a slow hand over her belly. "But I've been good and this is a bona fide emergency."

"Was that a yes?"

"Yeah. One cup."

They sat at the table not saying much, waiting for their aunt and sister. It didn't take them long. First Josie arrived and then Marilyn. They each grabbed her close and hugged her good and tight.

"Did you eat?" Auntie M demanded. Alex shook her head. "All right, then. Breakfast first."

Auntie M whipped up some eggs and Josie made toast. As they ate, Alex brought them up to speed on the West situation.

When she'd confessed it all, Payton said, "I love you. I understand why you couldn't say yes to him. But sweetheart, I know West pretty well now. If he said he loves you, he means it."

Auntie M put her work-roughened hand over Alex's. "I don't think it's Weston's sincerity that's the issue here."

"You're right. It's not." Alex swallowed down the lump of misery that had somehow lodged itself in her throat. "He wanted more and I don't have more to give right now." She glanced at Josie, who was pressing her lips together. "Say it, Josephine, whatever it is."

"Well, it's just that you make it sound like you *can't* give him more, that you're not capable of giving him more. I really think it's more that you're not *willing* to give him more."

Alex sat up straighter. "All right. I *won't* give him more right now. That's all there is to it."

Payton jumped in. "You're saying you don't love him and you don't think you ever could. Right?"

Hadn't she just been all through this, ad infinitum, with West? "Lovc is not the issue."

The meaningful looks went flying around the table before Josie said, "Love is *always* the issue."

Alex groaned. "No, it's not. And come on. You guys, with your good men and your happy-ever-afters. I'm glad for you. I really am. And I do know that West is one of the good guys. I know how great he is and I care for him. A lot. But I'm not there yet, okay? I have stuff to figure out and that stuff has to be my focus right now." She turned another glare on Payton. "I know that look. Something snarky is about to come out of your mouth."

"Well, I might have been about to remind you that it really is possible to walk and chew gum. But I won't do that. Because that would be mean—however, there is something important that I *am* going to say."

Alex tried not to sneer. "Of course you are."

Payton drank the last sip of her one cup of coffee. "You're lying to yourself."

She was not going to ask—but then, she did. "About what?"

"You're in love with Weston. We all know it."

"No. I am not lying. How many times do I have to say it? I *care* for Weston. A lot. But I'm not *in love* with him."

"And now you're lying about lying to yourself," Payton accused.

"You truly are pissing me off."

"Same," her sisters muttered in unison.

Auntie M only sighed. "We love you. We are here for you. Anything you need, we'll see that you get it—if we can. But I think what you really need is a good cry. And sadly, knowing you, that's most likely not going to happen."

"I've made my decision. West left. He and I are through. I miss him, but I understand why he had to go. What possible good is crying going to do me?"

Payton and Josie shared a weary glance, after which Josie replied, "A good cry would mean you're getting in touch with your emotions, getting closer to surrendering to what's really in your heart."

"Oh, dear God. You did not just say that to me.

As though I don't have any clue what's in my own heart."

"That's not what Payton said," Josie offered gently.

And Payton nodded. "I firmly believe that you do have a clue, you just refuse to acknowledge what you're feeling."

"I know exactly what I'm feeling, thank you."

"Oh, really? Then answer honestly—when was the last time you cried, Alex?"

"I don't remember. So what?"

"When your dad died?" asked Josie.

Alex pressed her lips together. No, she had not cried when her dad died, but why should she? When she was little, she'd cried a damn river over Leandro Herrera. All the tears in the world hadn't helped her one bit.

"So not when your dad died," Payton answered for her. "What about over Devon and his evil ways? Or that Rob guy?"

"This line of inquiry is getting us nowhere."

"The only time I ever remember you crying I was ten, I think," Josie went on as though Alex hadn't even spoken. "That would've made you twelve. Your dad had called to tell you he wouldn't be coming to pick you up, after all."

"He did that a lot."

"Yeah. He did." Josie's tone had softened. "But

that was the only time I remember you crying about it."

It had been the last time, too. After that, she refused to believe a word of it when Leandro called with big plans to take her to Disneyland or Universal Studios. Or just to his house in Beverly Hills, where he promised they would hang out together by the pool and he would take her to dinner at Lucy's El Adobe and Spago and Musso & Frank's. As long as she didn't believe, there was nothing to cry about when he called at the last minute to say he couldn't come see her, after all.

"All right, you guys," she said. "I appreciate the love and attention. I feel better already."

Did she? Not really, not deep down, not when she thought of West and longed to have him here, wrapping his arms around her, smirking at her, whispering naughty suggestions in the middle of the night. But she did feel comforted. And cared for. And that mattered a lot.

She pleaded, "Can we talk about something other than my absentee father and the emotional benefits of a good crying jag?"

For several uncomfortable seconds, they all three sat there staring at her. And then they shoved back their chairs and surrounded her. Josie took hold of her arm and pulled her up into a hug, which became a hug fest when Payton and Auntie M joined in.

When they let her go, she reassured them, "I love you guys and I do appreciate your showing up to make certain that I'm all right…"

Josie took the hint. "You want us to go."

"I just don't know what more there is to say…"

"We're right here," said Auntie M. "Whenever you need us—"

"I know. I love you."

Auntie M and Josie left.

Not Payton, though.

Alex closed the door and turned to her younger sister. "What now?"

"Well, I've been trying to decide the best time to tell you this…"

"Just say it."

"All right. Easton got West to promise he would fly back down on Christmas Eve, that he would have Christmas here, with the family."

"Of course, he should be here."

"Right now, Alex, I'm not sure about that. But at least Joyce will stay out of it as long as she knows we're all going to be together for the holiday. But all bets are off if West doesn't show up for Christmas. If he doesn't get down here, Joyce will have Myron driving the motor home back up to Seattle to find out what, exactly, is going on with him."

"Do you hear me arguing? He belongs here for Christmas as much as any of us. I get that."

"He can stay at our place," Payton promised. "We'll work it out."

"At your cottage, he'd have to share the boys' room or sleep on the couch. That's no good. He's already said he won't stay in the motor home, and nobody wants him all the way out at the Heartwood Inn."

"Aunt Marilyn has a guest bedroom at her cottage."

"And West will feel uncomfortable about moving in on Auntie M and Ernesto—no. The back bedroom here is empty. He should just stay here."

Payton had a look that said *you've got to be kidding me*. "I don't think so, Alex."

She stifled a heavy sigh. "I'm sorry. I really am. I've screwed everything up."

Payton just shook her head.

That night was a tough one. Alex missed West so much. She wondered what he was doing, if he was okay, exactly how much he hated her, if he would ever forgive her…

She had to get up and put her phone on the dresser across the room to keep herself from grabbing it and tapping out a quick text begging him to please come back.

By the next morning, she had a plan and the plan was called "structured activity." She kept busy helping out around the farm. She showed up at Auntie M's to pitch in with dinner Monday night. She took Cookie on long walks—too long really—and more than one per day. Miles kept the farm roads cleared, so Cookie never got stuck in the snow, but the little dog always grew tired before Alex was ready to go back to the empty cottage. She started taking along the doggy backpack West had bought, wearing it in front so it was easy to slip the mutt in and out.

Yes, it made her sad every time she grabbed the pack to go out for a walk. She would remember the fun they'd had, the three of them, those few days in Portland.

Not sad enough to cry, though. No way. Alex had nothing against anyone who cried when they were suffering. On the contrary, she respected that most people had that willingness to let the hurt come out. She simply was not willing and hadn't been for over twenty years.

Tuesday, she got a call from a woman who'd worked on *California Law Review* with her at Berkeley. Laine Reed lived in San Francisco, where she practiced family law.

Laine greeted her with, "Hello, Alex. It's been too long. And I had to call when I heard through the grapevine that you left KJ&T..."

They talked for over an hour—about burnout, about all the reasons a successful career woman might suddenly decide to try something different.

When Alex admitted she had no idea what she would do next, Laine said, "You're a powerhouse, Alex. Whatever you choose, we both know you'll be the best. And you were always so driven. At some point, you have to slow down a little—reassess, reevaluate. Figure out what makes your life worthwhile."

"So hanging around at the family farm is just what I need to be doing right now?"

"Essentially, yes."

Alex ended that call feeling better than she had since West walked out the door Sunday morning.

Better. But far from good.

She missed him. So much.

And already, not even seventy-two hours after he'd walked out the cottage door, she was starting to realize that she just might have made a giant mistake. She had a bad feeling that she'd blown it in a huge way—and not because she'd walked out on her big-time career. The bad feeling only got worse as each day crawled by.

Each of her sisters and her aunt took her aside separately. They asked her if she was all right. They wanted to know what they could do to help.

She lied. She promised them that she was fine, ordered them to stop hovering, stop worrying about her. They respected her wishes and backed off.

And that only made her feel even worse about everything.

On Saturday morning, which was Christmas Eve, she woke to someone knocking on the cottage door. She grabbed her phone to check the time. Not even seven yet. Outside it was still dark.

"What now?" she asked no one in particular, belting her robe as she answered the door.

Joyce Wright, in elf-pattered flannel pajamas, snow boots, a red wool hat and a big green puffy coat, stood on the welcome mat. "Sorry to wake you, Alex. But West called me a few minutes ago to say he's not coming down for Christmas."

Because of me. "Oh, no!"

The red pom-pom on her hat bounced as Joyce nodded. "We really need to talk..."

Alex ushered West's mom inside, made coffee and sat down with her at the table.

Joyce took Cookie in her lap. She scratched the little dog between the ears. Cookie huffed out a happy sigh as Joyce announced, "I'm not a fool, Alexandra."

"No! Joyce, of course you're not."

"I've seen you and my son together. I know what's going on. It's finally happened. And I couldn't be more thrilled."

"Thrilled about what?"

"Don't play dumb, Alexandra. We both know you are anything but. It's perfectly obvious. Weston is in love at last. With you."

"Well, I..." Her throat locked up. She coughed into her hand to clear it—and then spoke the truth for the first time out loud. "Joyce, I love him, too."

"Yes, I know you do." Joyce calmly sipped her coffee. "What I don't understand is what's gone wrong between the two of you. Why did he suddenly run back to Seattle? And why is he not coming to the farm for Christmas? Believe me, I'm accustomed to him going where he wants to go and doing exactly what he wants to do. But Christmas is sacrosanct. And Weston knows that very well. Is he being an idiot about this?"

"What? No! Joyce, it's not him, it's—"

"Alexandra, don't go easy on him. He always was the troublesome one. I love my boys equally, but the truth is, Easton made motherhood a breeze. Weston did not."

"Joyce, no. Listen. It's not West, I promise. It's me. I'm the problem."

Joyce gave Cookie a kiss on the head and set her gently on the floor. She leaned toward Alex. "What happened? Tell me."

And Alex told her. All of it. That West had said he loved her and that she'd turned him down. "And that's why he went back to Seattle. I'm sure that's why he's not coming for Christmas. Because of me. He doesn't want to be around me. He doesn't want to see my face." All of a sudden, her eyes were blurry. She sniffled as the first tear dribbled down her cheek. "Omigod." Carefully, she pressed her fingertips to her cheeks. They came away wet. "I'm crying. I really, really am..."

Joyce jumped to her feet, pulled Alex close and wrapped her up in soft, warm arms. She smelled so good, so comforting—of coffee and Chanel No. 5. "That's all right, honey." West's mom patted her back as she cooed in her ear. "Don't you worry. We will fix this. It's all going to work out just fine, you'll see." Joyce whipped a neatly folded tissue from the pocket of her elf pajamas. "Here now. Dry those big brown eyes and we'll talk about what you need to do next."

West's two-bedroom penthouse loft in Pioneer Square had it all—two thousand square feet on two floors and a fantastic rooftop outdoor space with a panoramic view of Elliott Bay. On a clear day, standing at the window wall that showcased the bay, he could see Bainbridge Island.

Too bad Christmas Eve day had started out gray and promised to stay that way. Dark clouds hung heavy in the sky over choppy waters, and drifts of last night's snow covered the outdoor chaises and tables. Staring out at the grayness did nothing to lift his bleak mood.

He wandered down to his living room on the floor below. Dropping to the polished concrete ledge by the fireplace, West braced his elbows on his knees and stared at the floor. He couldn't shake this glumness. It had hung on him like a wet coat, weighing him down since last weekend when Alex had made her position perfectly clear. She didn't want a future with him. She wouldn't even consider the idea.

He knew he ought to…

The intercom buzzer cut him off in mid-mope.

Who the hell could that be? He wasn't expecting anyone and he didn't want to see anyone.

The buzzer sounded again. Probably some street person, trying all the units, hoping someone would just let him in.

When it buzzed a third time, West had had enough. He got up and went to the box by the door. "Not interested. Go. Away."

"Let me in."

He knew that voice like he knew his own. "East?"

"Buzz me in. We need to talk."

West was waiting in the hallway when the elevator doors slid wide. "It's Christmas Eve. Are you out of your mind?"

East lounged against the elevator wall, his

heavy jacket slung over one shoulder. He straightened and emerged between the doors as they started to close. "You called at six in the morning and canceled on Christmas. That's a bridge too far."

West remained blocking his own doorway. "I woke up and decided I just didn't want to be there."

"Too bad." East came toe-to-toe with him and stopped. They stared each other down. "It's Christmas. You know the rules about Christmas. We all come to Christmas, no matter what. I haven't talked to Mom yet. That won't be fun."

"You don't have to explain anything to her. I called her, too. She knows I'm not going to be there. You don't have to worry about it."

"But I am worried about it. Somebody has to talk some sense into you."

"You shouldn't be here. This is insane."

"No argument there. Let me in." Shaking his head, West stepped aside. Easton handed him the jacket as he breezed past. "I had to pay Jason a small fortune to fly me up here. He's waiting at King County airport to fly back and the meter is ticking." Jason March lived in Hood River and flew the air taxi between Columbia Gorge airport and Seattle. He and Easton had struck up a friendship during the months East had run the renovation of the Heartwood Inn. "Let's get this settled so we can get going."

West scoffed. "There's nothing to settle. I'm not going anywhere."

East looked at his watch. "It's after nine. I'm hungry. Get me some coffee and something to eat."

West tried to think of the right words—the ones that would send his twin back out the door. Nothing came. When East made up his mind about something, there was no turning him around.

Finally West muttered angrily, "Eggs and toast?"

"That'll do."

West cooked the eggs and they sat at the kitchen peninsula.

East gobbled down the food before he spoke again. "You messed up. You know you did. And now you're acting like a big baby." He put on a whiny voice. "I'm not coming for Christmas. My *feelings* are hurt."

West considered punching his brother in the face. But he took the high road instead, announcing loftily, "It doesn't matter. She's not giving me a chance. We're done."

East dropped his fork hard enough that it clattered against his plate. "Dude. You surrendered the field. You were supposed to learn from my mistake. But you did it anyway—you broke the first rule of getting the one you want. Never. Surrender. The field." He paused for effect. West was about to tell him to put a sock in it when he went on, "However, I'm willing to cut you some slack on this. I get that you're a complete newbie at loving a woman and you have no idea what the hell you're doing. That's why I'm here, to offer a little guidance and a quick flight back to where you need to be."

"I don't need to listen to this sh—"

"West. You're a mess, I get it. But you wimped out on Christmas and that is nothing short of a cry for help. So here I am to do what needs doing."

"I'm not going."

"Yes, you damn well are. Pull it together. Pack a bag and let's go."

"She doesn't want me there. And I don't want to be there."

East took a gulp of coffee and set the mug down hard. "Yes, she does want you there—and you want *her*. Open your eyes. Alex may be my sister-in-law, but I hardly know her. I rarely saw her until she quit her job. Still, even *I* can see how much she loves you."

He didn't believe that, but damn. It did sound good. "Did she *say* anything?"

East gave a disgusted snort. "Are you kidding? She's cut everyone off. She's like a damn ghost, carrying that old dog in a backpack everywhere she goes. She keeps to herself, spends most of her day walking around the farm or cleaning stalls and grooming the ponies. And just like you, she refuses to talk about what happened between you two. She told Payton and Josie and Marilyn to stay out of it, that she didn't want to hear about it, didn't want to talk about it. Just like you."

He felt like crap that she was having a bad time—like crap with a side of hope. "You mean, you think she misses me?"

"How many ways can I say it? You're in love with her. She's in love with you. One of you has got to give. I'm here to help you with that." East's phone rang in his pocket. "It's Payton." He put the phone to his ear. "Hey, I'm here at West's and we were just..."

Payton said something from the other end of the call.

"Yeah?" East said that much too quietly. Now he was nodding. "Okay. I'm listening." Payton said something more. "Absolutely. Yes. Go, baby. I love you—I love you and I'll be there. Quick as I can." He stuck the phone back in his pocket. His face was pale. "Payton's in labor. She called from the car on the way to the hospital in Heartwood."

Chapter Twelve

West threw a few things into an overnight bag. They grabbed their coats and headed for the elevator.

Downstairs, East had a limo waiting. He barked instructions at the driver as they climbed in. "Back to the airport. Pull out all the stops."

That driver did not fool around. They exceeded the speed limit most of the ride, squealing around more than one corner. The six-mile drive took nine minutes and when they got to King County airport, the Cirrus G2 Vision Jet was waiting. They were in the air five minutes after boarding.

And if they didn't get there before East's little girl made her appearance, West would never forgive himself. Was everything okay? Damn, he hoped so.

The baby was due about three weeks from now. He was afraid to ask East if there was some problem—if Payton and the baby were all right.

West knew his twin. The look on Easton's face shouted *do not disturb.*

East stared straight ahead, his gaze out the windshield up front, as though he could make the plane go faster by the sheer force of his will alone. He'd missed the births of Penn and Bailey. It was a real sore spot with him, that he hadn't even known Payton was pregnant, that he'd had no clue he had twin sons until four years after they were born.

A half hour into the hour-long flight, still staring straight ahead, Easton said flatly, "She just *had* to come home for Christmas. But she's not *that* early. It should be okay. She and the baby should be fine." A low, growling sound came from deep in his throat. "She'd *better* be fine. They'd both better be fine. And we'd damn well better get there in time."

"We will," West said firmly, though he couldn't be sure and he knew it would be wiser at this moment to keep his mouth shut.

"You make it up with Alex," East muttered out of the side of his mouth. "I can't stand seeing her dragging around the farm, her and that sweet little old dog. It breaks my damn heart."

"East, I swear to you. I want to make it work with her. I want that more than anything."

"Changed your tune, have you?"

"I'm only saying, she needs to want that, too, and I'll do my best."

"Just make it happen. Or else."

West kept his thoughts to himself after that.

They landed half an hour later. East had driven Payton's SUV to the airport. They got off the plane and ran for the car.

West took the wheel and Easton called the hospital. He got to talk to Payton. When he hung up, West dared to ask if everything was okay.

"So far, so good," East replied. "Drive faster." A moment later, Easton actually looked at West. "Listen." His voice was gentler now. "I want you to be happy. I really do. And I know you love her. So I'm pushing you. It's for your own good."

At the hospital, West dropped Easton off and went to park.

When West got inside, he followed the signs to labor and delivery, where he found his dad and Miles and Ernesto in the waiting area. Miles explained that a nurse had already come and taken Easton back to Payton. Josie, Marilyn and West's mom were at Payton's side, too. Hazel and Ashley were looking after the twins at Josie's house.

Miles said everything was going fine. No problems so far. A nurse had just come out to give them a progress report. Miles rattled off something about dilation and effacement.

West stared blankly at Josie's husband and reminded himself that Miles was a farmer. He must have seen a lot of animals giving birth. Plus, he had two daughters and he'd delivered baby Davy. It made sense he would know all about having babies.

The good news was that everything really did seem to be going well and East had arrived in time to see his daughter born.

But where was Alex? Back at the farm with Cookie?

Even if his leaving had hurt her as bad as East seemed to think, wouldn't she want to be here for this? It really wasn't like her to stay away from any major life event involving her aunt or her sisters.

He turned to Miles to ask him if he knew where Alex was, but before he got a word out, his mom appeared from the hallway that led back to the delivery rooms. She rushed right to him.

"Weston!" she cried and then grabbed him in a hug the minute he got to his feet. "Oh, Weston. I'm so glad you're here."

His gut knotted. Something wasn't right. Gently,

he took her by the arms and held her away. "What's going on, Mom?"

She gave a wobbly smile. "Nothing!" She said it too fast and too frantically.

He held her eyes and kept his voice low as he insisted, "Talk to me. Tell me. What is it?"

His dad shot to his feet so fast, he shook the ornaments and tinsel on the small tree beside his chair. "Joyce?"

She flapped a hand at him. "Myron, sit back down. There is no emergency here. Payton's doing well, all the baby's vitals are strong and the doctor said it's almost time to push." His father didn't look completely convinced, but he did sink back to his chair. His mother turned to him again. "Weston…"

"For God's sake, Mom. Just say it."

"Well, I do need to explain a few things, that's all."

He frowned down at her. She was up to something, he could see it in her smile—so sweet and loving, but anxious, too. And she'd walked out of the delivery room where her first granddaughter was about to be born. No way would she miss a moment of that unless…

"Is this about Alex, Mom?"

"I promise you, it's nothing bad. Really. It's *good.* It's just…well, I only wanted to help. I had no idea that your brother would fly up there to talk some sense into you. And apparently, he got there before Alexandra did."

"There?"

"To Seattle, of course."

"Wait. Let me get this straight. Alex went to Seattle?"

His father was on his feet again. "What's this about, Joyce?" he demanded.

His mom blew out her cheeks with a big gust of breath and stared up at West pleadingly. "When you called me this morning, I felt I had to do something. So I dropped by Alex's house and we had a little chat."

"What?" barked his father. "Joyce. You went to Alexandra's cottage?"

His mom winced. "Yes, Myron, I did. You were still sleeping and I thought, why not just pop over there and have a little talk with her, see how she was feeling, find out more about, er, everything. And then when I got back, you were still in bed so I just started breakfast and—"

"Joyce." His father cut her off in mid-babble. "You didn't say a word. Not one word to me about this all morning."

"No, I didn't. Because Alexandra asked me not to. She said please not to get the rest of the family involved. She said that she needed to talk to Weston first. She asked me not to say anything to anyone until she called me and gave me the go-ahead." His mom's pleading gaze swung to West again. "She said that if you knew how she really felt, she might manage to convince you to come back to the farm. That way, you two could be on the road to Wild Rose together when she called to say she was bringing you home. And everyone would be so glad!" his mother cried. "And I..."

She was wringing her hands by then. "So of course I promised I would not say a word. And I haven't—well, not until now when it's obvious there's something of a problem. I was just going to call her myself, check on her, tell her that, as it turns out, you're already here in Heartwood. But then I thought, no. I should have a little word with you first to see what's—"

"Wait. You're saying that Alex is on her way to Seattle to see me, to get me to come back to the farm?"

"Yes. And she should be there about now, so I was just waiting on her call and she hasn't—"

"Hold on a minute." West's phone had just buzzed in his pocket. His heart rate lurching into overdrive, he whipped the phone out and saw he had a text from Alex.

I'm here. In Seattle. Downstairs in your building. I buzzed several times. You didn't answer. West, are you there?

* * *

His mother brushed his arm. “Weston, could that be Alexandra?”

“It’s Alex, yes.”

She slapped her hands against her mouth and immediately started talking right through them. “Oh, good. You need to…”

“Not now, Mom.” He turned and strode toward the reception desk. He loved his mother but he didn’t need her babbling in his ear while he tried to talk to Alex. He punched the call icon.

She picked up on the first ring. “West?” She sounded lost. And way too sad. “Oh, West. Where are you?”

His throat ached with all the things he needed to say. His eyes were wet, his vision blurred by hope and longing and the sudden, clear knowledge that things really might just turn out okay. “I’m right here.” He dashed the wetness away. “But, uh, not there.”

She laughed, the sweetest sound. “What?”

He heard a whine. “You’ve got Cookie with you?”

“Yeah. We, um, drove up together. West, I…” She sniffled.

“Aw, sweetheart. Don’t cry.”

“I just… I’ve been all turned around backward trying to figure out what to do with my life and that made it way too easy to lose sight of what I needed most. I've worked so hard, West."

"I know…"

"I pushed myself, drove myself relentlessly, to make my family safe, to be able, always, to take care of them, no matter what."

"I do know. I get it."

"And over the years, I just got in the habit of obsessing over work. It became a habit so strong I sometimes lost sight of *why* I was working, you know?"

"I do."

"It was always about making sure everyone's okay, everyone's provided for, that we never lose the farm. I put all my focus on building up my financial resources. And now, I don't even *need* to work, really. Not until I find out what I truly want to do. But still, I said no to you when my heart said yes and I screwed everything up. I freaked. I've never been afraid of anything. But this, with us…"

"It scared you?"

"Oh, yeah. West, I've been so afraid to trust this. So afraid it would all go up in smoke, like my marriage, like the thing with Rob. Like my dad, who was just never there and then went and died on me without my ever getting a single chance to convince him how much I needed him."

East had been so right. "I'm sorry I left you,

Alex. So sorry. I should have stuck it out, waited for you to catch up and believe I'm for real. Instead, I left you just like those other fools did."

"I was there, too. I pushed you away. And all I want now is to make it right and I… Look, if you could just buzz me in, if we could only talk, I'm sure we—"

"Alex, yes. We'll talk. I want that. We'll work everything out."

"Oh, I'm so glad! Buzz me in, then?"

"I would if I could. But I'm not in Seattle."

A soft, bewildered little laugh escaped her. "I don't… Then where?"

"Alex, I'm in Heartwood, at the hospital." She gasped. He rushed to explain the situation. "East flew up to talk some sense into me and then Payton went into labor and East and I flew back down."

"Wait—the baby's coming early?"

"Yeah."

"Is Payton okay? And the baby…?"

"Everything's fine so far. East and Josie and your aunt are in the delivery room with her. The baby should be here very soon."

"Oh, thank God. Where's Joyce…?"

He glanced back at his mother. His dad had his arm around her. She put on another crooked little smile and gave West a jaunty thumbs-up—

whatever the hell that meant. "She's fine. She just busted herself about sneaking over to the cottage to see you this morning."

"Oh, West. She's wonderful. She really is."

"She's got a big heart, that's for sure. And, Alex..."

"Yeah?"

"Come back to Heartwood. I want you here, with me."

"I will be there. Soon. It *is* Christmas Eve. Traffic hasn't been too bad. I might make it in under four hours..."

"I could meet you halfway..."

She laughed again, the sound lighter than before. "With our luck, we would drive right past each other—no. You stay in Heartwood."

"I don't want to let you off this call," he muttered prayerfully.

"I don't want to let you go either, but the sooner I get going the quicker I'll get there—and I'll check in with you on the way."

"I love you, Alex."

"And I..." Her voice trailed off.

His heart sank. "What is it? Just say it."

"It's silly, but the first time I say it to you, I want to be looking in your eyes."

"Not silly." The words sounded raw as he pushed them out around the tightness in his throat.

"Not in the least. Get in the car and get down here."

"I'm on my way." She hung up.

He turned to find his mother coming toward him. "Weston, is she all right?"

"It's good. She's good. She's coming back to Oregon now."

"Oh, I am so happy, so very relieved." She grabbed him in another tight hug and then stared up at him, breathless. "Well."

"What, Mom?"

"Nothing. Everything. I can see in your eyes that you two will work it out and I'm just glad, that's all. So glad—and I guess I should go see how Payton's doing. I'm really hoping to be there when our little girl arrives."

"Go."

Pausing only for a quick kiss from his dad, she headed for the doors that led back to the delivery room. West sat down beside his father.

Alex called half an hour later, checking in as she navigated her way past Tacoma. He had nothing to report, really. Except that the baby would be here very soon. It felt so good, to listen to her voice, to know that he would have her in his arms before the end of the day.

He'd just said goodbye to her when his mom came bustling through the wide double doors from the delivery room, a giant smile deepening the laugh lines on her face.

She went straight to his father, who rose as she came to him.

"Well?" his dad asked.

And she threw her arms around his neck. His dad lifted her right off the floor and spun her around.

"She's here!" West's mom announced much too loudly for a hospital waiting room. "Her name is Sofia Marilyn Wright. She's got all her fingers and toes and she's the prettiest little girl in the whole wide world!"

At ten past three that afternoon, Alex parked in the hospital lot, put Cookie on her leash and walked her to the building's main entrance.

West was waiting out in front as promised, a small suitcase on the ground at his feet. Alex's pulse started racing at the sight of him. He turned and saw her.

And she scooped up her dog and ran for him.

"Finally," he said as he opened his arms and gathered her in.

He bent to her and she lifted to him and when their lips met, her world, spinning out of control for months now, found its axis at last. Cookie wriggled with happiness and swiped doggy kisses at both of them.

When they finally let go, she handed Cookie to him and he stayed outside with her so that Alex could check on her sister and meet Sofia. Before finding Payton's room, she detoured to a restroom to wash her hands and splash cold water on her face. It felt good to freshen up a little after a long day on the road.

In the hospital room, the blinds were drawn. Easton snoozed in a chair next to Payton's bed. Payton, too, was sound asleep.

Alex crept close enough to bend over the bassinet and get a good look at the swaddled, sleeping baby within. As she watched, the little girl yawned wide and gave the sweetest, softest little sigh.

"Alex. At last," Payton whispered from the bed.

They shared a smile. Alex whispered back, "What a trip, Paytaytochip. You did good."

Easton stirred. "Hey. Alex." He got up. "Everything okay?"

"Everything is excellent, Easton."

"I'm glad."

She gave him a big smile. "And thank you."

Easton shrugged. "I caused more problems than I solved, but I meant well—and I'll give you two a moment." He kissed his wife. "I'll be right back..."

Payton patted the mattress as Easton left the room. "Come here," she whispered. Alex eased around the bassinet, rolled the bed tray toward the wall a little and managed to squeeze in next to her sister.

"What a day, huh?" Payton covered a yawn.

Alex had to agree. "Never a dull moment—well, except for the driving. That got old fast."

"Weston?"

"Outside with Cookie—I take it Easton brought you up to speed on the, um, situation."

"He did, yes. And what he didn't know, Joyce did."

"I love Joyce," Alex said. "She can be very motivating."

Payton laughed, but quietly. "That she can—and I just want to say that happiness is a good look on you, though I'm guessing you and Weston haven't even had a chance to really talk yet."

"We did, a little. On the phone while I was standing in the entry of his building and then later, during my long drive back."

Payton crooked a finger. Alex leaned even closer and Payton whispered in her ear, "What are you waiting for? Sofia and I will be back at Wild Rose tomorrow. You can start spoiling your niece then. For now, get lost."

Alex kissed her cheek. "Love you."

"Love *you*. So much."

West and Cookie were waiting right where she'd left them. She went out into the wintry afternoon, but then hung back for a moment to admire the man she loved. His shoulders were so broad and strong. His dark gold hair could use a trim, as always. And the rest of him…

Best-looking man she'd ever seen. Coming or going. Bar none.

Cookie, sitting patiently at his feet, turned her head and spotted her. Rising and stretching, the dog gave a welcoming whine.

West turned, too. Their eyes met. He gave Alex that incomparable smile of his, the one that lit up the gray day and made her wonder how she'd lived all these years without him.

She stepped in close. "Let's go back to the cottage." He dropped a quick kiss on her mouth, handed her Cookie's leash and picked up his suitcase.

At the car, she passed him the keys and got in on the passenger side. Cookie curled right up in her lap and went to sleep.

The fifteen-minute drive passed in silence. Alex tried to relax, but she had so much to say to the man beside her, so much she wanted him to know, so much to share. Her body seemed to vibrate with the need to tell him everything.

The cottage was just as she'd left it that morning, the tree alight in the window, the *Merry Christmas* welcome mat and the festive wreath on the door inviting them in. She paused on the walk to admire it.

West stopped when she did. "It's a great little house," he said.

"I'm always going to think of it as our Christmas cottage."

He grinned down at her and she grabbed his hand and pulled him up the steps.

Inside, she unclipped Cookie's leash. They took off their coats.

She was hanging hers on the peg by the door when he reached for her. The coat dropped to the floor. She let it fall. All that mattered was the feel of him, his scent of soap and spice, those strong arms of his around her.

His mouth covered hers and she moaned in delight—to be kissing him again, to know that he wanted her and she wanted him and they would make it work, the two of them, no matter what.

"Seattle," she said against his mouth.

He bit her lower lip and then licked the spot. "Yes, I'm familiar with it."

"And yes, West, I want to live there. With you, if that works for you."

"Yes."

"Just like that?"

"Just like that." He captured her mouth again, his tongue dipping in. As he claimed her lips, he walked her backward into the little hallway and two steps later, into her bedroom.

They fell across the bed together.

"All these clothes," he grumbled, breaking their glorious kiss long enough to get hold of her sweater. She raised her arms over her head and he whipped the sweater up and away.

Things happened fast after that. He peeled everything off her as she did the same for him. They were laughing between eager sighs and hungry moans.

His boots hit the floor one after the other, followed by hers. They were both sitting up at that point, both focused on getting naked, making it so there was nothing in the way, no slightest scrap of fabric to separate them. They tore off their socks and sent them flying. He shoved down his boxer briefs as she shimmied out of her panties, popped the hooks at the back of her bra and tossed it over her head.

He turned to her. They were both naked at last.

"Finally," he said low. And his mouth covered hers again.

They fell across the mattress, holding on tight.

"Now," she whispered, all urgency. "West, I just need you now..."

He grabbed a condom out of the drawer, freed it of its wrapper and rolled it on.

"I do want to have babies," she informed him as he rose above her.

"Me, too. Right this minute?"

She snickered and playfully slapped his hard chest with the back of her hand. "Soon..."

And then he was there, pressing close, filling her where she needed him most. She wrapped herself around him, grabbed the hard curves of his perfect butt and yanked him into her, good and tight. They groaned in unison as he filled her.

His eyes, deep and blue as oceans, held hers.

And she said the words that mattered most. "Weston Wright, I love you. I'm *in* love with you. I want you now and I want you forever. I do. I truly do..."

"You have me. I love you, Alexandra. I never thought I would find you, never even believed that there was someone just right for me. But here you are and yes, forever. I want that, too..." He took her mouth. Their tongues danced together, their bodies moving in unison, rising and falling in perfect rhythm. There was no more need for words.

She surrendered completely to her love for him, trusting him, *knowing him*, believing in him and all they would have together. A whole life to share, a future to build, the two of them.

He pushed in so deep. She moaned in sheer pleasure as she felt her climax gathering, tightening—and then opening up, spreading out from the core of her, until her whole body shimmered with wonder as fulfillment bloomed all through her.

A moment later, as she held him so tight, she felt him pulsing, filling the condom, groaning her name.

"Eat." West set a roast beef sandwich and a bag of potato chips in front of Alex, who sat at the kitchen island looking amazing in fleece sweatpants and his shirt. She'd gathered all that thick, dark hair into a low ponytail that trailed down the center of her back.

"Thank you. *So* hungry. I think you've depleted all my reserves." She dug right in. He poured her a tall glass of milk, made himself a sandwich and took the stool beside her. "We missed dinner at Auntie M's," she said once she'd gobbled down several big bites.

"So did East and Payton."

She grinned at him. "No one's knocked on the door."

"They've probably guessed we're busy."

"Very busy." She crunched on a chip.

He leaned close and stole a quick kiss. "Not through with you yet."

"I would expect no less." She sipped her milk. "I'm hoping they'll leave us alone until tomorrow morning—and I've been thinking..."

He made a sad face. "There's no thinking during reunion sex."

"Not during the sex, silly. While I was driving to Seattle and back. Plenty of time for thinking then."

"Ah. Had me worried for a minute there..."

"Well, don't be." She leaned her head on his shoulder. "While having sex with you, I never think about anything but how hot you are and how I can't wait to do it again."

"Fair enough. My manly pride is mollified." He took her hand, brushed off the salt from the chips and kissed her fingers one by one. "So tell me. What have you been thinking about?"

"I don't want a job, per se. I want to invest in small businesses, preferably businesses run by women."

"My girl, the venture capitalist. Sounds good to me."

"West, you're so *easy*."

"You're coming to live with me in Seattle. Before you know it, I'll have a ring on your finger. You're mine now. I can be pretty damn easy about all the rest."

Her brown eyes gleamed. "It might sound grandiose, but I want to help women live their dreams."

He turned on the stool, framed her face in his hands and kissed her. "Not grandiose."

"Really?"

"Yes. Really. It's who you are, Alex. You've always been there for your sisters and Marilyn. You're just casting the net wider now, that's all."

"I like the way you put that."

He kissed the tip of her nose. "What else?"

"Well, and babies—for right now, I just hope you'll think about us having babies."

"On it," he agreed with enthusiasm.

"I mean, we don't have to start setting the timeline for a family quite yet. We're not even engaged."

He was nodding. "We can practice making them—but with protection."

"Not sure it counts as practice if we're using protection."

Cookie whined. She stood by West's stool, looking up at him hopefully. He tore off a bit of his sandwich and gave it to her. She gobbled it up.

Alex said, “I love you, Weston Wright.”

He got down off his stool and grabbed her hand. “Come on back to the bedroom. You can show me how much.”

She laughed as he slung her over his shoulder and carried her to bed.

Epilogue

At ten Christmas morning, Easton brought Payton and little Sofia back to Wild Rose.

Everyone gathered at Payton's cottage. It was pretty crowded. Payton rested on the couch as they all jockeyed for a chance to hold baby Sofia.

Little Davy, just learning to walk, staggered from one piece of furniture to the next. He was learning to talk, too. "Hi there!" he exclaimed to anyone who smiled at him. He reached up his chubby arms to Miles and crowed, "Dada!"

Joyce corralled Penn and Bailey. The boys were bouncing off the walls to have their mom and dad home and to finally be allowed to tear into the giant pile of presents waiting beneath the tree.

As for their new baby sister, well, the boys decided to reserve judgment about her.

"She's so little," remarked Bailey warily.

"And her face is so red," Penn observed. "And she cries a lot."

West's dad took about a hundred pictures of the two boys sharing an easy chair with Sofia wrapped up like a big pink burrito between them. Myron got some good shots of Ashley and Hazel, too. They each got a turn holding the newest member of the family.

Except for Payton, Easton and Sofia, who rested at home, they all had lunch at Aunt Marilyn's and Christmas dinner at Josie and Miles's house.

West and Alex got back to their cottage at eight. He took her straight to the bedroom where they made love, talked and made love some more. It was one in the morning when Alex finally turned off the bedside lamp.

The next week was sheer heaven. They rang in the New Year together and on January 2, they headed for Portland, where they spent three days in Alex's apartment deciding what to donate and what to keep. They took Cookie on long walks and Alex discovered she had a certain nostalgic feeling toward the apartment now. It didn't bother her at all to be there. Because now she knew exactly where she was going next.

And she was ready when they got on the road again for the drive to Seattle. She loved West's place near Pioneer Square. They decided to stay there, at least for the near future.

By late April, Alex had put money into a woman-run start-up called NULAC, which engineered formula similar to mother's milk from bovine colostrum. When July rolled around, she'd invested more widely. She had a hand in a number of tech start-ups, a hair and nail salon opened by two women who had met in prison, and a pizza parlor owned and operated by a single mother of five.

West proposed in August. Alex shouted, "Yes!" as he slipped the ring on her finger. They opened a bottle of champagne to toast the moment.

Remembering their first night, West raised his glass to Leo, too. "Here's to you, buddy! I miss you and I wish you were here."

As for the holidays, they spent them in the Christmas cottage down in Oregon. And on New Year's night, Alex and West spoke their vows in the event barn right there at Wild Rose. The bride was three months pregnant. They'd already chosen a name—Leo or Leonie.

After their first dance, the cake cutting and

the bouquet throwing, she took her husband's hand. "Our carriage is waiting."

His eyes lit up. He knew where this was going, but he pretended not to have a clue. "Which carriage is that?"

"The wedding carriage pulled by two fine white horses." She moved in close and slid her hands up to clasp around his neck. He felt so right pressed against her—all man. *Her* man. Leaning up, she whispered in his ear, "Time to go."

"But where?"

"Back to the cottage—I mean, it's a wedding, right?"

He continued the game, frowning, looking baffled. "Well, yeah…"

"Are you saying you don't remember what we do after a wedding?"

"Hmm."

"Weston. After a wedding, we do it. Now."

West threw back his golden head and laughed. And then he scooped her up in his arms and carried her out into the clear winter's night.

* * * * *

Watch for an all-new series starring the next generation of Christine Rimmer's beloved Bravo family.

Book 1 is coming in March 2023 only from Harlequin Special Edition.

COMING NEXT MONTH FROM

HARLEQUIN®

SPECIAL EDITION™

#2947 THE MAVERICK'S CHRISTMAS SECRET

Montana Mavericks: Brothers & Broncos • by Brenda Harlen

Ranch hand Sullivan Grainger came to Bronco to learn the truth about his twin's disappearance. All he's found so far is more questions—and an unexpected friendship with his late brother's sister-in-law, Sadie Chamberlin. The sweet and earnest shopkeeper offers Sullivan a glimpse of how full his life could be, if only he could release the past and embrace Sadie's Christmas spirit!

#2948 STARLIGHT AND THE CHRISTMAS DARE

Welcome to Starlight • by Michelle Major

Madison Mauer is trying to be content with her new life working in a small town bar but is still surprised when her boss-mandated community work leads to some unexpected friendships, including a teenage delinquent. The girl's older brother is another kind of surprise—and they're all in need of some second chances this Christmas!

#2949 THEIR TEXAS CHRISTMAS MATCH

Lockharts Lost & Found • by Cathy Gillen Thacker

A sudden inheritance stipulates commitment-phobes Skye McPherson and Travis Lockhart must marry and live together for a hundred and twenty days. A quick, temporary marriage is clearly the easiest solution. Until Skye discovers she's pregnant with her new husband's baby and Travis starts falling for his short-term wife. With a million reasons to leave, will love win out this Christmas?

#2950 LIGHTS, CAMERA...WEDDING?

Sutter Creek, Montana • by Laurel Greer

Fledgling florist Bea Halloran has banked her business and love life on her upcoming reality TV Christmas wedding. When her fiancé walks out, Bea's best friend, Brody Emerson, steps in as the fake groom, saving her business...and making her feel passion she barely recognizes. And Brody's smoldering glances and knee-weakening kisses might just put their platonic vows to the test...

#2951 EXPECTING HIS HOLIDAY SURPRISE

Gallant Lake Stories • by Jo McNally

Jade is focused on her new bakery and soon, raising her new baby. When Jade's one-night stand, Trent Mitchell, unexpectedly shows up, it's obvious that their chemistry is real. Until Jade's fierce independence clashes with Trent's doubts about fatherhood. Is their magic under the mistletoe strong enough to make them a forever family?

#2952 COUNTERFEIT COURTSHIP

Heart & Soul • by Synithia Williams

When a kiss at a reality TV wedding is caught on camera, there's only one way to save *his* reputation and *her* career. Now paranormal promoter Tyrone Livingston and makeup artist Kiera Fox are officially dating. But can a relationship with an agreed-upon end date turn into a real and lasting love?

YOU CAN FIND MORE INFORMATION ON UPCOMING HARLEQUIN TITLES, FREE EXCERPTS AND MORE AT HARLEQUIN.COM.

HSECNM1022

SPECIAL EXCERPT FROM

HARLEQUIN

SPECIAL EDITION

Madison Mauer is trying to be content with her new life working in a small-town bar but is still surprised when her boss-mandated community work leads to some unexpected friendships, including a teenage delinquent. The girl's older brother is another kind of surprise—and they're all in need of some second chances this Christmas!

Read on for a sneak peek at
Starlight and the Christmas Dare,
the next book in the Welcome to Starlight miniseries by USA TODAY *bestselling author Michelle Major!*

"I'm going to call my friend who's a nurse in the morning. She's not working in that capacity now, but she grew up in this town. She'll help get you with a good physical therapist."

The warmth she'd seen in his eyes disappeared, and she told herself it shouldn't matter. It was better they remember who they were to each other—people who had a troubled girl in common but nothing more.

She couldn't allow it to be anything more.

"You need a Christmas tree," he said as she started to back away.

"I didn't see any decorations in your house."

He nodded. “Yeah, but Stella made me promise I would at least get a tree.”

“I’ll consider a tree,” Madison told him. It felt like a small concession. “Although I’m not much for Christmas spirit.”

“That makes two of us.”

Once again, she wasn’t sure how to feel about having something in common with Chase.

He cleared his throat. “I have more work to do—meetings and deadlines to reschedule. I can make it back to the bedroom.”

“I’ll see you tomorrow.”

“I’ll be here.” He laughed without humor. “It’s not like I can get anywhere else.”

“Good night, Chase.”

“Good night, Madison,” he answered.

The words felt close to a caress, and she hurried to her bedroom before her knees started to melt.

HSEEXP1022